BETWEEN FLIGHTS

BETWEEN FLIGHTS

Leighton D Geller

CCCProductions

To Chloë, the best sister a girl could have;
To Chance, who made me a mom; and
To Caledon, who is the best part of my
every day

PART ONE: THE BACKSTORY

1

PROLOGUE

Fifteen moving boxes. All packed with the contents of my two-bedroom condo. All labeled and taped shut. The boxes didn't include the furniture, of course, or the numerous garment bags and trash bags filled with my clothes and shoes. Instead, they contained kitchen items, office supplies, and other odds and ends. How was all of this going to fit into Mason's house with all his furnishings already there?

We had agreed that we wouldn't use just "his stuff" or "my stuff" and that we would blend all of our things and eventually decide what to keep and what to purge. We joked that we would have the most well-stocked kitchen ever, each already owning all the requisite appliances. With my fortieth birthday only months away, I had become accustomed to my favorite pan for cooking eggs, the blender with only one speed, and the mismatched glassware from pubs all over the world. But, what I also knew, was that of the two of us, I was more likely to assimilate into his world, then he into mine. That, over time, I would come to like whatever egg pan he used, that my blender would find a shelf in the garage, and that my pub glasses would likely make their way to the basement bar area.

Mason was three years older than me and had never married. I had dated more than him in my lifetime, but then, I had done a lot more of everything than him in my lifetime. Travel, living in different cities, diverse careers, moving far from family. He was adventurous, but his adventures included new chef-inspired recipes with hard-to-source ingredients, finding rare art pieces at auction, and playing on his guy's softball league. He brought calm where I brought energy. He paused before he answered a question; whereas, I spouted off the words as they entered my brain, usually in random fragments.

I shocked him one day when he found crumbs in my bed, "You eat in the bedroom?" Unabashed, I commented, "Yep, and sometimes in the bath."

To him, I was new territory, wild by his standards. To me, he was established, ruggedly handsome, and comfortable in his own skin.

Some friends had expressed concern with my move to the suburbs, sacrificing my quick subway ride to work each day, in exchange for a commuter train with a preset schedule. But the move made sense. Mason's job was half an hour in the other direction from the house, making his relocation to the city impossible. And I had sold my condo at the height of the market, giving me the funds needed to co-own Mason's home. Our home.

"And you are willing to give up everything after dating only a year?" a friend had asked recently. Until her question, I had not considered it as giving anything up, but as gaining something new. But her month-old question nagged me. So, I paused the packing and grabbed a can of beer from the near-empty fridge. On the counter was a magazine, leftover from an airport lounge from last week's business trip. The magazine, the beer, and I went onto the balcony for a much-needed break.

People-watching from the balcony. I would definitely miss that. With the opened beer wedged beside me in the wicker chair, I flipped open the women's magazine to its headline article, "Do You Date or Mate?"

The article, written by someone with unknown credentials, suggested that the surefire way to determine if you were a serial dater vs. someone who was destined to settle down was to reflect on your past dating life. The author suggested making a list of all your past relationships, even the ones dating back to your teenage years when wearing someone's sweatshirt at a bonfire meant you were dating. The list, she claimed, would allow you to see the type of men you were drawn to, where you found happiness, and whether you could be content with a mate, or if you preferred a life of perpetual dates.

For as long as I can remember, I have made lists: to-do lists, lists of places I'd hoped to travel to, pro-con lists, shopping lists. Not all were memorable. They weren't framed or treasured in a drawer. No, they were the day-to-day lists that find themselves crumpled in the bottom of my purse or forgotten in the pocket of a pair of jeans, only to be found later in the dryer's lint trap.

These lists have changed over the years. In the pre-teen years, they were more dreamlike and charged with optimism. I remember when I discovered "My Future Jobs" written on flowery paper in immature handwriting. It was in a box from my parents' basement with "Re-bekah's Childhood" scrawled on the side in thick black marker. Apparently, dog sled driver, cruise ship activity director, and goodwill ambassador made the top of the list. I am not even 100% sure what I meant by goodwill ambassador or how I ever expected to become a dog sled driver, living in a major city in North America. Yet, there they were, staring back at me in purple and pink ink. (I have to admit, I might have enjoyed that cruise ship gig.)

The pro-con lists came later. These lists covered the gamut of job offers, moving, and other such weighty matters. I even made a pro-con list once of owning a dog, losing all rational control over the subject on the day I went to the shelter "just to look" and came home with the best decision ever.

While I was all about making lists, I usually scoffed at articles like these, deeming them more entertaining than insightful. But this one struck a chord. Did I tend to date instead of mate? I had to admit, that was a valid question. While I was with Mason now and definitely on the path to "mating," I felt like this list would give me some closure on my past relationships and my friend's nagging question, while helping me make space for this next chapter in my life.

Besides, I figured one more list couldn't hurt.

Another sip of beer and I was in search of paper and pen. The closest thing to paper I could find were those thin sheets of packing paper that come with the moving boxes, for wrapping fragile items. It would have to do. I titled my list "THE MEN" in bold letters with the sharpie. I even threw on a few hearts and drew confetti and streamers, as I pondered where to start.

***

Later that week, the move went smoothly. Nothing appeared to have been broken and most of the items, except for the clothes, were piled neatly in the garage, awaiting unpacking over the coming days and weeks. We both had agreed that unpacking didn't need to be a one-day blitz. I figured it was a good omen that all my furniture fit. We placed some of my furnishings in the living room and a few statement pieces in the front hallway and the upstairs loft bedroom.

Mason had graciously given me the entire walk-in closet in the master bedroom and the larger dresser. He had already made a new home for his suits and casual clothes in the bedroom closet down the hall. The bathroom vanity, with its double sinks, had room for all our personal items. And there was a heart that Mason had drawn on the mirror in erasable marker that read, "Welcome Home, Rebekah." I found it endearing and searched for my phone so I could take a selfie.

After unpacking the essentials, we lounged in the backyard under the elm branches. Mason had put ribs on the BBQ to simmer for tonight's dinner. A few of my friends and another couple would be joining us later. The couple were friends of Mason's from work who lived about three blocks away. I'd met them at a company fundraiser a few months prior. I liked them and found them very similar to us: She was outgoing and loud, like me. Whereas, her partner was more reserved and reflective, like Mason. I knew they'd love my college friends Lexi and Nick, who married years ago, as well as my best friend Olivia, who'd recently separated.

Shortly before everyone was due to arrive, I was on a mission to find my glass pitcher so I could make margaritas for everyone as a housewarming drink. I had a pretty good idea what box it was in—one of the last ones I'd closed up—so I wandered out to the garage armed with a knife to saw through the packing tape. Feeling my way through two boxes, I found my pitcher in the third one. Triumphant, I returned to the kitchen with the pitcher and glasses and almost ran into Mason with the knife still in hand.

"Whoa there! No stabbings on moving day, please." He said smiling.

"Sorry," I laughed. "I was just digging out the margarita set, so I could whip up a batch before they get here."

"Salt-rimmed glasses? Let me help," was his response as he reached for the glasses, still wrapped in packing paper.

The ingredients for the margaritas were all on the top shelf of the fridge, exactly where I'd placed them when I stocked the fridge the weekend prior. I was slicing a lime and singing the words to the song coming from the kitchen speakers when Mason said, "Rebekah...what is this?" With my back to him, I wasn't sure if he was asking about the song or if I hadn't brought in the right pitcher after all. I smiled and turned to him with lime juice dripping off my hand.

His face was pale, and he was holding the crumpled packing paper, having just unwrapped the glasses. Immediately, I could make out the heading in bold sharpie, the hearts and the first few names written in pen. It was the list. Used at the last minute as packing material, as I dashed to get the remaining few things in order before the movers arrived.

I swallowed. Then words started racing out of my mouth—about the article, about my penchant for making lists, and most importantly, why I made the list. My words had a pleading tone, as if I were trying to make the whole thing sound mundane. From his expression, Mason found it anything but.

"These are men you had relationships with?" he asked, as if trying to cement his understanding. I nodded.

By now I was rinsing the lime juice off my hands and carrying on with the mechanics of making the margaritas. But my mind was racing. We had, after a month of dating, had a fleeting conversation about past relationships. I had been brief and had glossed over most of my history, intentionally asking probing questions of his past to steer the conversation away from my own.

It was a mistruth by omission. He was likely left with the impression, after that conversation, that I had a handful of exes, like he did. A total not requiring more than two hands to count out. He had no idea I had been married before, maybe twice, or that I'd lived with other men in the past.

I had skimmed over my dating narrative on that occasion because Mason and I had just started dating. I figured if it was an important topic, it would come up again. But it never did. It was not embarrassment or remorse over my past that made me keep quiet about my past. It was more that men quickly associated a history like mine with someone who did not want to settle down and this was something that could not be further from how I felt about Mason and our relationship's trajectory.

As Mason unfolded the crumpled paper and moved items from the counter so he could press the pages out flat, he counted and read the comments. I looked away. To make the list, to engage my memory, I had put salient points beside each name: where we met, how long we dated, something noteworthy about our relationship, and how it ended. I hadn't gone so far as to assign ratings to each but had numbered them with a tally at the bottom, before ultimately using the list to wrap the glassware.

The pitcher of margaritas, ready, was now in the fridge, as if highlighting a celebration that was now canceled. I busied myself with cleaning up the kitchen as I saw Mason leave the room. With the list.

I heard his car start and pull out of the driveway. There were no screeching tires, just a calm departure as the black sedan passed out of my view beyond the hedge. Soon after, the doorbell rang. The first guests had arrived.

I busied myself greeting everyone. Olivia was the first to arrive with Mason's colleagues walking up the driveway just as I was reaching to close the front door. I thanked everyone for their gifts of wine and flowers and introduced Olivia to the young couple. We were on a tour of the main level when the doorbell rang announcing Nick and Lexi's arrival. Mason's absence weighed heavily on me and added to the awkwardness I'm sure my guests were also feeling. As soon as they walked in, I blurted out that he was running an errand. Like if I said it fast enough maybe it would be true.

Nick and Lexi eagerly joined the tour of the upper level and gushed at my new abode. While I tried to conceal my shock over Mason finding the list, they were beaming with excitement over my new relationship status. As we went from room to room, I smiled and did my best to play the gracious hostess. But inside I was kicking myself. Why did I have to make that list?

After the tour, I suggested we all sit and have drinks in the backyard, so I could steal away from the group and check in on Mason. While I was grabbing the margaritas, I texted him to see if he was OK and to let him know the guests had arrived.

While we were sipping our drinks, I tended to the simmering ribs on the grill. From what I could tell, they seemed OK, but I have to admit, I'm not the best when it comes to grilling. When Mason's colleague, Asher, offered to take over the BBQ duties, I readily accepted. I engaged in light conversation about the blooming perennials in the neighbor's yard that were peeking through the fence rails. I refilled everyone's drinks and mixed up a second batch of margaritas, stealing Olivia away from the group as an impromptu helper. While we were making drinks, I told her what had happened with Mason. We whispered in hushed tones in the kitchen, and I texted Mason again. I asked him to text me back, just so I'd know he was safe. I thought of asking if he wanted me to send the guests home, but I decided to wait. I didn't want to overload him while he was still processing everything.

When we stepped outside with the drinks, Lexi offered a playlist to fill in the awkward silences that were forming. Nearly two hours had passed since the guests first arrived. Mason's absence could no longer be excused as an errand. Olivia helped me carry out the salads and side dishes that Mason had prepared. As I arranged the dishes on the outdoor dining table, Olivia motioned for the guests to take a seat. Before passing the potato salad, I decided it was time to give up the charade. Looking directly at my guests, I told them what had happened: the magazine article, the list, Mason's reaction, everything.

While I waited for them to respond, I set the bowl down and took a long sip of my drink. I told them if they felt uncomfortable and wanted to leave that I would completely understand. To my surprise, everyone was extremely understanding and offered to stay. Cora said she was sure he would be back soon. Asher texted Mason, to "check in." And Lexi said she was starving and started to fill her plate.

While everything smelled great, I could only pick at my food. Olivia, noticing that I was preoccupied, whispered that she would stay until Mason reappeared. She then asked me, with the others hearing, if I wanted to talk about the list. Friends since our teens she knew me. I did my best processing out loud. By telling the stories, she knew I might figure out how I had gotten into this predicament. At first I was reluctant to share such personal details with Mason's colleagues present, but when I saw how receptive everyone was, I was starting to warm up to the idea. I looked down at my phone. Still no sign from Mason. Olivia leaned her head lightly on my shoulder for moral support and Lexi, sensing my hesitation, topped off my drink.

I looked around the table at each of the guests. Who knows? Maybe Olivia was right. Maybe it would help to get things off my chest. Eyeing my margarita, I took a sip and set the glass down. Since Mason had the list, I had to go from memory. Unsure of where to begin, I decided to just start with the first story that came to mind.

PART TWO: THE MEN

2

NUMBER EIGHT

Guy number eight was adorably sweet.

He was a year younger than me. We'd met on a train to Paris while he was traveling with two high school friends. I was traveling alone and struck up a conversation on the train while it was still at Waterloo station in a deliberate attempt to engage with them.

I remember asking, "Which way will the train be going?"

"To Paris," one of them responded.

"To the coast," the guy beside him said.

And then there was guy number eight. There was something different about him. He simply said, "Out of the station." I liked that response. It was succinct and mysterious at the same time.

At the time I had no idea I would become intimate with one of them. It certainly was not my intention. They were enjoying their first taste of freedom after high school graduation in Kansas. And I was on the longest journey of my life up to that point: a three-month stay in London with mini explorations around England and a trip to Wales. My last couple of weeks before returning home to my second year of college was a week-long trip to see the highlights of Western Europe.

The Eurorail pass—it was every backpacker's best friend.

***

I'd left my luggage in storage in London and traveled with just a daypack. It was similar in size to what kids carry to school these days. Never again would I travel so lean. While it was exciting to be out on my own at such a young age, back then my life didn't include all the beauty products and wardrobe changes that it does today.

That summer's adventure was my first solo trip, taking place just three months before my nineteenth birthday. With it came the challenges of independence right alongside those of navigating a foreign land.

Looking back, it was pretty amazing that I decided to go to Europe on my own. I didn't have an adventurous upbringing. The trips with my family included a long trip where we drove to Disneyland when I was a kid and got to see the West Coast. And there were some trips I went on with my high school to Boston, Florida, and Mexico. Of course, there was the little foray into freedom on those high school trips, but nothing adventurous. While we were highly supervised, those trips instilled in me a deep love for travel that I've carried with me ever since.

The planning stage of the Europe trip had included four of us. Me, my best friend at the time, and two other girls, one of whom floated on the periphery of the group. As the date approached my best friend bailed. While she had good reason (she stayed home to work in her parents' store), I was disappointed. And my other friend had to bow out, because she didn't have the money for the plane ticket. That left me and the peripheral-girl I barely knew: Leslie.

Undaunted by our brief history, Leslie and I embarked on the trip abroad. I quickly learned she was a little more delicate than I was, as she didn't roll with unplanned events as easily as I did. Setbacks in our transportation, our room arrangements, and jobs that were promised (but never materialized), caused her great grief and many phone calls home. Whereas I called my parents when I'd first arrived and then again on day three to tell them about my great rented room and my new job at the Hard Rock Café, something I'd stumbled upon when I stopped for lunch while job hunting.

I made fast friends at the restaurant and quickly grew tired of my moping roommate who was always shopping for new clothes, but somehow seemed to keep wearing mine. At some point in our three months together she met a Londoner and thereafter spent little time in the house, for which I was both grateful but also a bit worried.

Eager to experience London to its fullest, I engaged in activities with my newfound work crew. We went to concerts, bars, and rugby matches. We even went to Wimbledon. I also ventured to Wales for a brief trip, returning to work a few days later. When I eventually quit the job and said my goodbyes, I knew that feeling of freedom that travel offered had captured me.

Leslie and I didn't cross paths again. That was just life. It was something even my almost-nineteen-year-old self understood. She dropped out of college to stay with the Englishman she met. At the time, her decision seemed illogical to me and short-sighted, but also very romantic. Those very reflections bolstered me to chat with the three boys that I'd heard speaking "American" on the train to Paris.

***

Before the train even pulled out of the station, I'd moved and was seated in their quad, exchanging travel stories. Their adventure was just beginning. They had a multi week itinerary through Europe and were overly excited that I spoke French, a level of fluency that I grossly exaggerated. They declared me their interpreter while we were in France. I beamed inwardly, knowing that I'd just met my travel companions for my Paris adventure.

After a four-hour journey on the train, we each awoke to screeching brakes as the train entered the station. Keith and I were covered in a blanket, something he must have retrieved from his bag while I was sleeping. An unspoken connection had developed from sitting so close to each other. One of his friends appeared nonplussed, and I chalked it up to him not being happy that a girl had invaded their "guy trip." It never occurred to me that he might be disappointed that I didn't choose him, something he shared with me at the end of our trip.

Our adventures were your typical tight-budget tourist stuff. We took pix of each other at the Eiffel Tower and got kicked out of more than one greenspace for walking on the grass and tossing a frisbee. We purchased bread, cheese, and wine and picnicked in the park. And we sat by the Seine and saw the city lights. We also went to expensive restaurants and ordered appetizers and water, much to the chagrin of our waiters. And we laughed and stayed out until it was almost time for the city to wake up. In short, we lived.

The youth hostel we stayed in separated the men from the women, so I was in a different wing than my traveling companions. During our five days together, I was routinely met by Keith in the lobby as we planned our day. On day four, I was greeted by Keith's friend, the standoffish one, and he told me the boys were going to do something on their own that day.

While I hid my disappointment, I would have likely planned my day better if I had known. I popped back to my room to grab some essentials for the day and returned to the lobby shortly thereafter to explore the city on my own. Passing through I saw Keith and his friends, each filling up their thermoses with coffee. I waved and continued out the building.

A few minutes later Keith caught up to me outside.

"Where ya off to?"

I said I wasn't sure, but if their plans didn't include dinner, perhaps we could meet up later.

"What plans?" he asked.

"Your guy plans, the stuff you guys are doing today."

Keith looked puzzled. "I don't have plans with them today. I was hoping to spend the day with you."

He proceeded to explain that he told the guys that morning to do something on their own, because he was going to ask me to spend the day with him. Alone. Upon realizing the intentional mix-up, he didn't even return to the lobby for his thermos or to inform the guys.

Our day began right then.

We walked the back streets of Paris from the hostel toward the Louvre. We talked. We held hands. We had no set destination. As we walked, we described our home-towns and the lives we were returning to in the coming weeks. He shared that his former girlfriend at home had a pregnancy scare that year. Whereas I shared that I was worried I wouldn't actually get on my plane to go home.

We ate bread and cheese and sipped wine by Pont Neuf, admiring the city in the distance. We made love in a park in the middle of the afternoon, and he told me he could think of no other girl his age capable enough to travel alone. At the time I hadn't thought much of it, but over the years I'd heard similar comments and began to realize I had different priorities than most.

Two days later, all four of us were at the train station. I was headed to Italy, and Keith and a friend were headed to Amsterdam and the friend-not-chosen was scheduled for a later train to join them.

Keith and I engaged in a movie-style kiss goodbye on the platform and he said, "You are the kind of girl a guy could fall for. And change his plans for."

I remember saying something like, "Don't change your plans for anyone. Especially me."

Then he asked me to let him know if his other friend tried to hit on me once he left. He said honesty and loyalty among friends were paramount to him. I promised I would let him know. Keith and I had our last-kiss scene by the train door as the uniformed conductor looked at us with disdain.

A few weeks later, after I had returned home, I was greeted with a postcard with a picture of the Eiffel Tower on it, postmarked from Kansas. It simply said, "Love Keith." I wrote him back and asked about his trip and how it was to be home and thanked him for my Paris adventure.

As promised, I advised him that his friend did try and change my opinion of him. The friend had said, "You should have chosen me. All the girls pick me over Keith."

To which I responded, "not all the girls" and laughed awkwardly.

Keith and I wrote a couple of letters back and forth, and then the letters stopped. Years later, when Facebook surfaced, I looked him up and sent him a message. He was married, with young children, but remembered me right away. I asked how his friends were, the ones I'd met in Paris.

He said he never saw that one friend again, once the European vacation was over. Keith said the parting of ways might have happened naturally anyhow, but he saw no reason to continue a friendship with someone who tried to "ruin Paris." We both agreed the trip was a special time. After that Facebook message we never communicated again. Some things are just better that way.

3

NUMBER ELEVEN

Guy number eleven was a friend of Madeline's.

Madeline lived across the street from me growing up. I'd lived there my whole life, and she moved there when we were both about seven years old. Her sister was a year younger than me and Madeline was a year my senior. We spent as much time in each other's homes as we did in our own, and I don't think I have a childhood memory that Madeline was not part of.

Their family, with all four daughters, went to a different high school than me, despite us living mere yards apart. This allowed for a different pool of friends, separate parties, and unless an effort was made, we didn't see each other in social circles.

I'd heard that Madeline was going to a party one fall and asked her to take me along. I returned the favor that winter, and she came to a few events at my high school. Madeline was a stunner. Gorgeous. The kind of girl that didn't know her own beauty and every guy in the room would try and talk to her. She had this sophisticated calmness about her that made her seem much older than she actually was.

One afternoon I was watching TV with her during our pre-teen years in the basement of my childhood home. My older brother, who was in college and saw Madeline as another sister, joined us. Not long after, my brother's girlfriend, Serena, came to the house and wandered into the basement to look for him. Serena saw him sitting on the couch with Madeline and me, and she couldn't believe Madeline was my friend. She thought for sure that Madeline was their age. Looking back, it's kind of funny. But at the time Serena was not amused.

One summer weekend, sometime in our late teens, Madeline was going to a cabin with some friends and invited me along. I remember there being an uneven number of girls and guys and no one was paired off.

I was introduced to the group and the host Sebastian. It was his parents' cabin. I remember it being very rustic in appearance, with just bare-bones furniture. There were three bedrooms, separated by those accordion folding doors, and seven of us. Sebastian got the master bedroom. That was a given, both out of respect for his parents and his repeated reminders to us that he was the host. I was assigned the couch and didn't mind in the least. I was just glad I didn't have to sleep in the not-so-screened-in porch with the mosquitoes.

When we got there we took a boat ride. Sebastian and one of the other boys took turns at the wheel. This was back in the day when boating wasn't considered driving, and, as foolish teenagers, most of us were drinking beer aboard. Madeline was her usual reserved self, seated in the boat in her one-piece bathing suit with a tank top and shorts over her suit. There was a life jacket nearby her, hanging onto one of the molded fiberglass handles of the boat behind the driver.

I had asked her beforehand whether she was crushing on anyone in the group, and she told me she did like someone and named one of the boys, whose name I have since forgotten. I remember encouraging her to talk to him, but she was hesitant to do so. It was hard for me to understand how someone who looked like Madeline would ever struggle to get any boy she wanted.

Soon after, we stopped at a local shop that was accessible from the water and bought more snacks, beer, and cabin essentials. Just the novelty of arriving at a store by water was a highlight for me. I remember it being hot, the sun was out, and after gunning it to the store on the way there, the ride back was, in contrast, rather peaceful and calm. I was in the bow of the boat with another girl and Sebastian was driving. This was long before the obsession with sunscreen, when we used to be happy if we got a bit of a burn and considered it healthy color.

I don't know what came over me. Maybe it was the beer, or the sun on my face, or the fact that I didn't know anyone, but I took my bikini top off and looped it through my bikini bottoms to keep it from flying overboard. There I was, perched on the padded bench with just my bikini bottoms, a baseball cap, and sunglasses in the bow of the boat. My ponytail was flapping in the wind from the opening in the back of my cap, and my legs were dangling through the boat rungs off the bow.

I turned around briefly to gesture to Madeline to come forward and was met with her signature glare. Disappointed, she chose a rear-facing seat so she wouldn't have to look at me.

For all my encouragement to Madeline to live life and have fun, she had an equivalent repertoire of speeches for me about appropriateness and restraint. While I knew she disapproved, I held my position until the dock came into view, when I slipped my top back on.

While I sensed Madeline was upset with me, she never said anything beyond, "You couldn't get a tan with your top on?" once we got back to the cabin. It never occurred to me that Madeline might be jealous of my carefree style, despite her looks and overwhelming maturity.

In spite of the tension between me and Madeline, it was a typical cabin weekend among high school kids. We battled over card games and built wooden towers of Jenga. We drank canned beer, swam in the lake, and roasted unhealthy foods over an open fire. The boys regularly threw one of the girls in the water. Laughter replaced shrieks, followed by threats of retaliation.

On the second day, while it was still daylight, with the group dispersed in various tasks of prepping dinner or chopping firewood, Sebastian approached me and asked if I was interested in taking a walk. Dressed in shorts, my favorite faded T-shirt and sandals, I agreed.

We walked in the woods for a while, and then he stopped and said, "Let's go this way."

I willingly followed. I stumbled at one point on the path, and he reached back, grabbing my arm to steady me. The path wound around some tall trees and ended at another cabin.

When he stopped in front of the cabin, I asked, "Who lives here?"

Sebastian said it was his uncle's cabin who only used it a few times a year. He pulled a key from his pocket and unlocked the front door. I smiled, with a rush of excitement. We went inside, and he gave me a quick tour. It was smaller than the one belonging to his parents, but much more modern in its furnishings.

We sat on the deck overlooking the lake, as he produced two beers from the back room. They were only slightly cooler than room temperature. We chipped off the frost that had built up on the sides of the ancient freezer to chill them in a bucket beside us. Since we'd been gone awhile, I asked if the others would wonder where we were. He said he'd told one of the other guys where we were headed, so I relaxed further.

After we finished our beers, Sebastian took me by the hand back into the cabin. We both knew why. We walked to the kitchen, and he gently lifted me onto the counter. We made out with increasing intensity and discarded our clothing, a piece at a time, discarding it into a heap on the floor. Sebastian reached into the pile and pulled a condom from his front shorts pocket—the same pocket that had housed the key to his uncle's cabin.

I nodded. It was a hot connection. Chemistry hot, but also sweaty hot. It was quick but uniquely satisfying. We kissed a bit afterward. Then we got dressed and walked back to his parents' cabin. Just before reaching the cabin he turned to me and said, "This isn't only once I hope, Rebekah. Can I can call you when we are home?"

"I'd like that. Just ask Madeline for my number," intentionally requiring Madeline to consent. Giving him my number would be the deciding factor on whether she wanted me to date Sebastian.

Before we went inside, I asked him, "You brought condoms to the cabin. Did you plan on sleeping with someone up here? Those are your friends, aren't they?"

To which he replied, "I didn't *bring* condoms. I *bought* condoms. That was why we suddenly needed to go to the store, despite having everything we needed already."

His response made me feel instantly at ease. Even though I had enjoyed the encounter, it felt more special knowing that it wasn't a planned event and that he actually felt something for me.

That night, while I was asleep on the couch, Sebastian woke me by gently touching my hand. I was wearing only a ragged T-shirt I saved for sleeping. I woke easily and followed him, throwing on my shorts before we went outside. We walked down to the water silently and sat on the dock, dangling our feet in the dark water. We did no more than kiss that night, or the rest of that weekend, but it was very sweet and sexy. And secretive.

***

We dated for a few months after that. (Madeline did give my number after all). Our dating consisted of a few trips to the movies, watching TV at each other's homes, and a few dinners out. But mostly it was sex. He was surprisingly well informed and patient about showing me new moves. He even introduced me to porn flics. Up until then porn was a bad word in my mind meant for swingers or men on business trips who watched dirty movies in their hotel rooms. But with Sebastian, I discovered it was more mainstream and available in a separate section of the video store, where XXX plastered the walls and you had to show ID to browse the selections.

I stayed over most Friday nights at Sebastian's house, leaving before his parents got up in the morning. Our sleepovers went undetected, until the morning his dad met me at the front door as I was leaving and offered me pancakes. The meal was delicious, and the conversation was surprisingly fluid. His parents, in turn, asked me about my plans for the day and some questions about my family. Mostly it was surprising because it was so casual and calm. We all knew I had just shared a bed with their son the night before yet no one seemed to express any issue with it. I was both grateful and surprised. Sebastian took it all in stride as he shoved huge forkfuls of pancakes into his mouth.

After that, Sebastian and I saw each other on week-days, usually meeting up for a meal and quick encounter in the back seat of a car or a friend's couch before heading to our separate homes. Then, after a few months, Sebastian and I just stopped calling each other. It was mutual. I think we both realized much of the glue in our relationship was sex, and the connection became weak. We didn't dissect it or try to patch it. We just let it dissolve and parted naturally.

Five years later while I was out with Madeline one night, we reminisced about old times. When the subject of that summer at the cabin came up, she told me that Sebastian and I likely had broken up, because she'd finally gotten the nerve to call him and tell him how she felt about him.

She said she was in love with him at the time, and when he found out he eagerly reciprocated. I hadn't seen that coming. But looking back, now I get why the topless boat ride had upset her so much. Finally, Madeline had gone after what she wanted. Good for her.

4

NUMBER
THIRTY-THREE

Guy number thirty-three was a coworker.

Through the latter part of high school and all during college, I worked part-time in an office tower that was walking distance from home. In the evenings and weekends I worked for a major banking corporation. It was an interesting experience. Let me just say, there's a lot that goes on in an office during the off-hours in work and personal spheres. You may think I'm exaggerating. But I'm 100% serious. What I've seen and experienced would surprise most people.

I'd been working at the bank for almost five years and was in my graduate program after college. I'd since relocated to the city and was in my first little apartment in a safe neighborhood. The lengthy subway commute to work did not dim my joy of city living. It was contract work, and, in the summers or during breaks in school, I'd work full-time during the day. That particular summer the work was in the accounting department and, yes, it was as dry as it sounded.

My personal quadrant of hell was located on the fourth floor, just one floor down from every other department I'd ever worked in. It was one floor down from the group that had known me since high school. One floor down from where I'd worked full time the previous summer, and one floor down from anyone who was even remotely close to my age.

My boss for the summer, a woman named Bertie, was known for having "no time." She had no time for questions, no time for mistakes, no time for my socializing, and no time for my humor. She was a well-respected woman at the bank and was skating toward retirement, fast. I tried to stay under her radar while I performed my meaningless tasks that paid astonishingly well for someone my age.

On a typical day, I moved numbers into different columns, added up expenses, and attached the calculator tape with the totals to the reports. I also volunteered for anything outside the ordinary just to break up the monotony. Anytime Bertie looked at me over the top of her thin silver-rimmed reading glasses, I knew that I'd better find something to busy myself with, or I'd be in for another lecture about the laziness of my generation. On one such occasion, I volunteered to deliver the mail for the accounting department.

Mail delivery involved collecting a bunch of boring invoices, expense reports, and other documents that needed to be distributed to the department managers in the building. I had to hand-deliver them to make sure the intended recipient signed for them. Bertie had never lost an invoice on her watch, a record she planned to keep until her retirement. And she reminded me of this regularly.

I delivered mail to the entire eight-floor building. Usually, I could stretch my tour out to about ninety minutes. It only took me about an hour, but I didn't rush. While it wasn't an exciting task, it was nice to stretch my legs and not be looking at the boring stuff I was distributing. Bertie never said anything about the duration of my deliveries. I think she was just as glad to be free of me during my rounds as I was to be free of her disapproving looks. So, it was pretty much a win-win.

That summer, my brother's wife, Serena, was profoundly pregnant and had invited me to their home to try on all her business clothes. She'd temporarily outgrown her stellar wardrobe that she wore to her job at an advertising agency in the city. Up until that point, my part-time positions had been jean-friendly, but daytime work required something a little more sophisticated. I had interchangeable outfits that had been in the rotation since last summer, so her invitation to broaden my wardrobe at zero expense was most definitely welcomed.

Since I hadn't lost any precious documents during my rounds, Bertie decided to add mail delivery duties to my regular task list. It was around this time that I started putting my new classy wardrobe to use. At first it was more subtle, a stylish blouse paired with my own pants or my skirt paired with Serena's fuzzy cashmere sweater and statement necklace. Bertie noticed and commented one day when she saw me in the ladies' room adjusting the waistband of a pencil skirt.

"Dressing to impress, I see."

I nodded as I adjusted my skirt.

Apparently, she approved, because she then said, "It's important to dress for the job you want, not the job you have."

Granted, while the venue was not ideal, this was probably the longest personal conversation Bertie and I had that whole summer.

As excited as I was about the clothes, I was thrilled that my new undertaking took me to the fifth floor each day. I made my circuit around the same time daily. I would glide through the fifth floor shortly after 11 a.m. I'd timed this strategically so my friends would not be away on break or at lunch, increasing our odds for "co-incidental" chats at the photocopier, a meeting point where nothing of importance ever got copied. My female friends would comment on each other's outfits, and we'd joke about sharing outfits between us before Serena needed them again.

What I didn't realize, or really contemplate, was that it wasn't just my fifth-floor female friends who were notic-ing. A group of young male customer service reps would time their duties so they'd be at their desks whenever I stopped by. There were six of them. They took turns stopping me to ask an accounting-related question, most of which I couldn't answer. A couple of them had girlfriends, but it was all in good fun. My longest visit was under ten minutes.

My favorite outfit drew a lot of attention, so I didn't wear it often. It was a knee-length white, business-style dress that hugged my hourglass shape well. It had black cuffs on the short sleeves with a black tuxedo-style collar and black buttons down the front. It was very similar to one that Julia Roberts had worn in *Pretty Woman*, my favorite movie at the time. I'd wear it with a set of black and white extraordinarily high heels that could have caused a stellar fall and much embarrassment. I even had to walk slower, as the contoured dress didn't allow enough room for a normal stride.

The first time I wore this outfit to the fifth floor, I walked deliberately and purposefully with my head held high, carrying the ever-important accounting paperwork to the customer service manager. I had a slight smile on my face and engaged in extended banter with the manager for no material reason. I nodded to a friend at the end of a row while she was engaged in a call and walked around to the far door leading to the elevator without stopping for socializing. I made it back to my desk just before lunch, in time for Bertie to ask me to help her with something.

That day was the first time someone from the fifth floor came to me. Daniel, someone I recognized from the customer service department, walked up to my desk shortly before 4:00 p.m. that day. I was already packing up to go home. The folks in accounting were very strict about adhering to our schedule and avoiding overtime. It was an unspoken pact. Daniel seemed a little breathless as he approached. I figured he was looking for Bertie, who'd just stepped away.

He said with a noted exhale, "Wow, this is where you are. Someone told me it was the *third* floor, and I just spent the last twenty minutes going from desk to desk there."

I laughed and said, "Is there something you need?"

After he caught his breath, he said, "I finish at four-thirty. Did you want to grab a drink?"

Now, it should be well stated that this banking tower had a favorite bar. And Calvin's, across the street, was the great leveler of our times. Executives, interns, managers, and mailroom clerks all chatted there without pretense, and no one ever talked seriously about work at Calvin's. Everyone was seen as equals. It was a place where you were pretty much guaranteed to run into someone you knew—or wanted to know.

While we were chatting, I told Daniel I'd be at Calvin's and that I was, in fact, headed there that minute. A snap decision I made as we were talking. Before heading over, I changed out of my dress into the clothes I'd worn that morning on the subway into work. All joking about Serena's wardrobe aside, I had ultimate respect for clothing and knew the white dress was not meant to meet messy underground transit.

There were about ten bank employees present when I arrived. I intentionally chose a spot with no spare chairs around me and chatted amicably with a few people from the fraud department. The fraud group and I had played together on the company softball team the previous summer. It was your basic small talk. There were the general inquiries about that year's upcoming event, including who was going to play and who was going to fail miserably, as well as speculation about who was going to pass out drunk before dinner.

I hadn't seen Daniel walk in, or sit down, but I looked up when a new round of drinks appeared at our table. I wasn't sure who had sent them. I figured it was probably one of the executives. But when I quickly searched for the sender, Daniel raised a glass and winked at me.

I'm pretty sure I turned about fifteen shades of red when our eyes met. You see, despite my experience with the opposite sex and my comfortable nature with guys, it always surprises me whenever someone picks *me.* I guess it's because I relate more to the inexperienced female outcast in the movies, where the cute guy waves to her, and she turns around to see who's behind her. Just like in the movies, I'm puzzled whenever I learn I'm the one on the receiving end of an affectionate gesture.

The group started to splinter away around 9:30. The plates of deep-fried-everything had long since been cleared away, and people were starting to turn down refills of their drinks. Many, like me, had to work in the morning. However, most, unlike me, lived nearby. I noticed Daniel had stopped his drink refills around 7:00, around the same time a few chairs became free near me, and he moved to my end of the table.

At first we chatted about our jobs and my boss (whom everyone knew of). He asked if Bertie was as tough as all the rumors. I demurred, but he pressed on, so I gave him some blanket statements like, "Yeah, she's a hard task master." He wanted to know more, but I changed the subject. So, we talked about current events and general office talk, nothing too deep, and all topics included the others around us.

A little before 10:00 I went to the restroom with another woman from the office. Once we were inside she turned and commented to me in a hushed voice, "I think Daniel is into you."

I smiled, thinking she was a little late with the breaking news but decided to play along and said, "Really? How do you figure?"

She then told me she'd heard from her boyfriend's cousin, who happened to be Daniel's closest work friend, that he'd been asking about me and whether I was seeing anyone.

"Interesting," was all I said. I had a feeling our conversation would potentially trickle back to Daniel, and I wasn't taking any chances on coming off too eager.

When I returned to the table, nearly everyone had cleared out. Not just from our section, but from the bar as a whole. Daniel held my jacket out to me. I wasn't sure what to make of the gesture. It was not in the chivalrous gesture of holding it for me to put on; he merely held it out for me to take, which seemed counter to his romantic gesture earlier in the evening when he'd sent some drinks to my table. Before heading out, I surveyed the table for lost and forgotten items. I hadn't paid for anything, nor did I even see the check, but that was not uncommon for the banking crew at Calvin's.

Without prior discussion, Daniel and I waited at the light and crossed over the busy road together. He was headed for his car in the garage, which is when he mentioned he lived about thirty-five minutes away. I, on the other hand, was headed to the subway, back through the office tower lobby. My trek would take me the same amount of time as his, but in the opposite direction, deep in the heart of the city.

Now that we were alone, my mind started to speculate, will he try and kiss me? Will it be awkward? I mean, we did have to see each other at work after all. At the dividing point, where I was to veer down the set of stairs to the subway and he was to veer to the parking elevator, Daniel said to me, "You weren't still planning to go home, were you?" And I got that wink from him again.

I didn't play all innocent and ask, "What do you mean?"

I also didn't act coy and say, "Why? What did you have in mind?"

Instead, all I did was blush again, all fifteen shades of red. And instead of taking the stairs, I pressed the button for the parking elevator.

5

When I woke in his parents' home it was quiet. The night before Daniel had mentioned his parents and sister were at their summer home. My mind was still a bit foggy from alcohol and not enough sleep. But the realization that I'd just slept with someone whose family had a summer home was starting to surface. I wasn't sure what to make of that, so I decided to shelve it under stuff to think about later.

Fortunately, we had enough time to shower. When I stepped out in my towel, he handed me a couple of headache tablets as he sipped his coffee. When I mentioned I couldn't show up in the same dress I wore the day prior, he took me to his sister's room and told me to pick out whatever I liked. While we were practically the same size, I decided a dress would be the easiest and most forgiving size-wise. Thankfully my heels went with most items in her wardrobe. I settled on a burgundy wrap dress that was a tad snug and a tad long. Looking at the selection, I asked how old his sister was, and Daniel yelled from the other room, "She's sixteen." And I laughed. Of course she was.

Having found the hair dryer in the upstairs bathroom, I arrived in the kitchen with freshly dried hair. I didn't have on any makeup, but, thankfully, I had some in my desk at work and could put some on before Bertie came in.

When Daniel came back in the room he didn't say anything along the lines of "You look great" or "I had a great time last night." It was simply, "Are you ready to go?" At the time I thought it was a bit aloof, but I didn't give it much thought. We were both rushing to get ready for work, and there wasn't time for things like flattery.

We could have showered together. I'd even suggested it, but he said it would only have gotten things started again, and we needed to get to work. He was right. Showering would have led to sex, and we *did* have to get to work. While I would have loved to have started things up again, pragmatism won out, and we showered separately. On the way to work we agreed he would let me out on the side of the building at the subway entrance to avoid arousing suspicion, and we'd chat later in the day. There was no kiss goodbye, but I did hear, "Have a great day!" before he sped off in his navy blue hatchback to the underground garage.

I made it to work on time and went straight to the restroom to freshen up before my day started. My morning was pretty uneventful. In fact, Bertie was not even in, so I was a little bored and not really pushing the limits of my abilities. I was also pretty nervous. Nervous about my rounds with the accounting documents. The mail delivery rounds that brought me such joy, the occasion to visit my friends and swing through other departments, were hampered by the fact that Daniel didn't seem warm and fuzzy that morning. Perhaps he wasn't a morning person. Or maybe he was having regrets. It was too early to ruminate, and the accounting paperwork waited for no one. So, as a good summer student, off I went, right on schedule.

I lingered in the other departments longer than usual and stalled further at the opposite end of the customer service floor, away from Daniel's desk. I laughed loudly at someone's not-so-funny joke. By appearances, I was having the time of my life in the snug borrowed dress.

I started my trek toward the other end of the office, where the manager sat and I stopped, deliberately, pretending I was reorganizing the documents, as if I didn't have a care in the world. When I quickly glanced to the left while I handed over the documents to the manager, I noticed that Daniel was not at his desk. Perhaps my lingering killed any chance for a visit. My insecurities resurfaced, and my mind turned in many different directions, none of them positive. Fortunately, I was jolted out of my thoughts when the manager handed me back the signed papers and undaunted, I headed quickly to the glass door to continue with my route.

"Rebekah!"

Some guy called to me and caught the glass door to the elevator just before it closed. When I heard my name, I pressed the close door button a few times. I wasn't really in the mood for company after missing the opportunity to chat with Daniel.

After the elevator door reopened, I saw that it was Drew, the one the girl in the bathroom the previous night had been referring to. Was this the cousin, the friend of Daniel's?

We rode up a flight together. Eager to get away, I stared quietly at the shiny elevator door, hoping he would do the same. As soon as the elevator doors opened, I stepped out and then heard him say, "Rebekah, right?"

"Yes," I nodded, unable to avoid him.

Then he handed me a white, sealed envelope and said, "Daniel got called into a meeting but said to give you this. Man, you walk fast. I looked up and saw you and then went to get this, and then you were gone!"

Embarrassed by the unwanted attention from the on-lookers in the hallway, I quickly thanked him and walked away. I carried the envelope with me for the rest of my deliveries, not daring to open it until I was back in the boring sphere of accounting. At my desk, Bertie had left me a voicemail with a few instructions on some assignments she had for me. Since I'd taken longer than usual with my rounds, I immediately set out to complete the assignments, my own secret penance.

Just before lunch, I opened the handwritten note.

"Nice dress," was all it said, along with a smiley face.

It was not a gushing display of affection, nor was it washing instructions for his sister's clothing. I liked the note and liked that it was a compliment without even having seen me. I decided to accept it for what it was and not ruin it with my usual overthinking.

***

About two months later, Daniel and I were still seeing each other, staying regularly at my apartment in the city. We'd started hanging with Drew and Isabel who were known as the "power couple" of the fifth floor. On my accounting rounds to the other floors, other cliques of my friends were asking how life with Daniel was. Word got around it seemed—way faster than my floor-to-floor mail delivery.

It was a great summer of patios, visits to Calvin's, and playing in the bank's baseball tournament. After the tournament Daniel and I wore only our baseball jerseys during a weekend getaway at his parent's empty summer home.

It was your typical couple stuff. We met each other's friends and shared the commute to work most days, but we made no long-term plans. By October, our connection was dissipating. I was back in college, so my schedule at the bank dropped to part-time, including some evening shifts. I also wasn't hanging out at Calvin's anymore during the week. I regularly asked Daniel to join me at various campus events on the weekends, but he always politely declined.

Around Halloween Daniel and I parted ways, amicably, but it was still sad. I cried as I hung up and considered making one of those desperate calls, asking him to ignore my breakup. Instead, I chose to go where my two BFFs were gathered watching cliché slasher flicks. My friends knew things were waning with Daniel, but I hadn't told them that I had ended it with him.

So, I decided to just rip off the band-aid, and when I walked into the darkened rec room where everyone was watching the latest victim getting chased in the woods, I decided to keep it light and asked everyone while I was taking a seat, "Hey, guess what I lost?"

And one of my friends looked right at me and said, "About 185 pounds?"

And the band-aid was off.

***

I bumped into Daniel a few times after that at work events. And about two years later, *two whole years* after the last time I saw him, I ran into him one night at Calvin's. I had been there on a date, a date that was not a match, and Daniel was with a group of the bank crowd, nearby. My date ended, and I didn't have the energy to join the rowdy group. So, I went to the restroom after gathering my things.

When I came out, Daniel was waiting for me near the double-doored entryway. He'd certainly had a few drinks. I, on the other hand, had decided to stop at one drink, trying to make a good first impression.

I studied him for a moment, perplexed.

"I can't drive my car home," he announced.

And I just looked at him and said, "Good call."

Pleading he added, "Can you drive it for me? Maybe to your place?"

I nodded. While he was not my forever person, he was good-looking in a quirky, tall, ginger sort of way. And it was just what I needed after all the awkwardness from the date I'd just had.

Turns out it was just what he needed, too. The chemistry between us was palpable. As we were walking to the parking garage, he stopped and pulled me close to him and whispered in my ear, "I remember you really liking sex. Is that still true?"

I responded with a passionate kiss. Both of us had everything untucked, and he had lipstick all over his neck by the time we reached the car.

On the drive home I ignored his intoxicated ramblings about how much he missed me and regretted breaking up with me. I smiled, keeping my eyes on the road. That was not how I remembered it, but I let him have that memory. I didn't want to kill the mood or the promise of good sex.

Just before we reached my apartment, while I was trying to parallel park his car on a packed downtown street, he said, "Do you still have that dress? The Julia Roberts one? Man, we all scored that dress a 10."

The randomness of his question threw me. It turns out the customer service guys had been scoring my outfits. I guess I should have been upset for being objectified in that way, but in truth, I was flattered. I was actually impressed that he still remembered that dress, and how I looked in it, a whole two years later.

And that dress did deserve a '10'.

6

NUMBERS FORTY AND FORTY-ONE

A New Year's trip to the Dominican Republic brought me guy number forty. He was nine years my junior. Before you judge me, you should know I was at the height of my running training, participating in as many as four half-marathons a year. I was in the best shape of my life, and my youthful face allowed me to carve ten years off my age. So why wouldn't I capitalize on that?

I was freshly divorced and had recently moved into my new home. My career was thriving, and I was finally making enough to spend money on myself. I had a killer wardrobe, a great car, and a close circle of friends. In short, everything was lining up, and I was ready for my next adventure.

It was my first time taking a vacation since my divorce. I had a renewed confidence and was happy with my choices in life, but I was also painfully aware that I was alone. I had yet to know this trip would be the relaunch of my solo travel career, something I would come to need later on as much as oxygen itself. Yet, on this trip, all I could do was smile politely at the other guests and hope that people weren't talking about me sitting by myself in the lobby or spending time checking my email after dinner instead of lounging with someone.

It was day two of the trip, and I had yet to muster up the courage to say, "table for one." I had eaten some food, of course. I grabbed something at the pool snack bar, from the gift shop, and a hurried breakfast on my way to the beach. But nothing that required a table or a reservation. Nothing where I would be noticed.

It was on that couch in the lobby, on day two, that I emailed my brother: *I think I made a mistake in coming here.* And his response was, *You have to eat! Go join people! When have you ever been shy?* I shut off my tablet and quietly tapped my foot in time with the lobby musicians, trying to seem like elevator music was just my sort of thing. My attempt to be social lasted another twenty minutes before disappearing to my room.

Day three was my first day out with others. There was a snorkeling trip scheduled on a party boat named The Calypso. I figured I would heed my brother's advice and join the group. Before I could chicken out, I hopped in the minivan that arrived at the hotel and said a hearty "hi all" when I boarded. I was wearing a purple polka-dot bikini with a white slip dress over it. And my bag held just the essentials: my wallet, a bottle of sunscreen, snorkeling gear, and my disposable underwater camera.

The van made the requisite stops at nearby hotels and the seats began to fill up until a joyful voice in Spanish-accented English came over the loudspeaker and announced we were now headed to the boat dock. Our guide gave us useful suggestions on what to do once we arrived, including where to present our voucher and where to meet after the trip.

I was quick to board the boat. I wanted to get settled and didn't stand around chatting people up. I simply got my stuff and climbed aboard. The boat had bench-style seating along the edges. At the bow it had one of those nets where you could sit suspended above the sea, if you were inclined to get your tan on. And there was another area downstairs with tables and chairs and a toilet. I decided to sit on deck and sat next to a couple from Toronto on the port side of the boat. We chatted about our Caribbean experiences thus far. It was apparent this couple, not much older than me, were tough to please. They were nice enough, but they moaned about the wait to get on board, the uncoordinated itinerary, and the lack of commentary from our guide about the sights around us. The couple even declined a welcome rum punch from the circulating tray. They seemed unusually rigid for the type of tour we were on, but they slowly warmed up. By the time we anchored at the first snorkel stop, we were chatting and pointing at sea life.

I had tucked my white cover-up in my beach bag once I'd discovered the sun was above our half of the boat. I had generously applied sunscreen to as much of my body as a single person could do and politely asked the woman sitting next to me to apply it to my back. In later years, I would come to realize that my back was the easiest to burn as a single traveler without a sunscreen buddy.

After the lengthy ride, I was eager to jump into the clear turquoise water. The Toronto couple were still fully geared up in shirts and shorts and wide-brimmed hats. The woman leaned over to me and said, "I can watch your stuff while you swim. I'm not going in. You never know what the staff do while you are off the boat."

Inwardly, I was appalled. First, because I don't think the staff would make much money, or keep their jobs for long, if word got out that they stole from guests. But it also upset me, because she assumed that they would steal, just because they were not from North America. However, I was not about to try and teach her different on this trip. I just accepted her offer to guard my gear and lined up at the ladder to step off into the ocean.

I could see from the people who'd gone ahead of me that the water was only waist deep. And it was at the ladder that I met number forty. He held out a hand for me at the bottom step, but I declined it. Once I was in the water, he asked whether I was traveling with the couple on the boat. Once he learned that I'd met them on board, he looked relieved and said, "They seem tight-assed. She didn't even get into her bathing suit."

I muttered, "I don't know. Maybe she doesn't like the water." And he just shrugged, dismissing my polite attempt to defend someone I'd just met.

We chatted near the ladder, exchanging names and resort info. He was Jim, and I learned he was staying at the same resort as me, but in a different section.

Pretty soon I broke off the chatter. This was a snorkel trip, and I'd just realized my time was being spent at the ladder. So, I dove off, leaded to the reef nearby where a crowd had gathered. I was hoping for a nice dolphin dive but plunged a bit too deep for the conditions. My camera, secured to my wrist, connected with my forehead during my swim. I surfaced some distance away, hoping no one noticed and praying it didn't leave a mark.

The boat's whistle sounded sometime later and we all made our way back to the boat. Jim magically reappeared and asked me to join him and his pal on the netting up front. He was cute, but I said no. I felt I should return to the couple who'd watched my stuff while I was gone. It didn't seem right to abandon them.

On the ride back I noticed him looking back from the netting to catch a glimpse of me every so often. The attention made me feel warm inside.

Disembarking at the dock was a bit trickier. The boat and the dock were not level with each other, and where it was a step *down* to board, it was a big step *up* to get out. Just ahead of the couple from Toronto, I knew Jim and his friend were behind us, and I wanted to keep my thirty-five-year-old self together. I stepped up, accepted the assistance of the crew member's arm, and bounced on the dock above with such a skip it looked like perhaps I was a pole-vaulter in my spare time. I surprised even myself. But my moment of glory was short-lived, because as soon as I was admiring my prowess, the couple from Canada pointed out, to everyone, that I'd left all my stuff behind.

After a chain of passengers handed me my items, while we waited for the bus back to the resort, Jim told me they always went to the resort's piano bar in the lobby each night just before dinner. I took that as an invitation but played it cool and just nodded.

The bus ride back was uneventful, and I spent the remainder of the day at the pool. As my accommodation was in the adult-only section, the pool was quiet, and the bar was blissfully obliging. I think I floated and stood in the water for four heavenly hours, getting out only to use the restroom.

7

After dipping my toe in the waters of single life on the snorkeling trip, I was getting the hang of solo traveling again. I made a reservation that night at the Italian restaurant just off the main bar. I finally had worked up the courage to have a real meal. By myself. And I wasn't going to half-ass it either. I refreshed my hair and makeup and put on a pretty, silver, backless dress. It was summery but also had a hint of sheen to it. I loved how it hit me mid-calf. I wore it with silver heels that were surprisingly comfy. Before heading downstairs, I took a quick look in the mirror and smiled. While I was a little nervous as I looked over my shoulder to inspect the back of my dress, I was totally rocking the beachy chic and felt I could do anything.

After confirming with the host, "Yes, it's just me," a few times, I was seated at a table for two, facing the restaurant's entrance. The bar was on my left, and there was a long table, set for ten, on my right. The second set of cutlery was whisked away from my table as if the mere sight of it might make me use it as a weapon.

I'd chosen the early seating for dinner. When I arrived I was the only guest in the restaurant. To pass the time,

I asked the waiter for a beer, calling it by the local brand name. When it arrived, I asked politely if my glass could be bottomless. I believe I used the term "ever full." I gestured to the top of my glass to solidify my point. The waiter smiled, tapped me politely on the shoulder and said, "Of course, Miss." I gave him $20. While it was primarily to thank him for keeping my glass full, I firmly believe anyone who calls you Miss at age thirty-five deserves an obscene tip.

I'd gone over the meager menu with such concentration, I could have recited it from memory. I tried to appear like dining alone was customary for me. I fantasized that I was a wealthy author, or benefactor, and decided I was making remarkable progress from the previous two days.

I was on beer number two and appetizer number one when the party next to me trickled in. It appeared to be a number of people in their mid-forties with kids in their late teens. And there was an older man who sat at the head of the table. I heard them call him "Pops."

I pretended not to be watching their evening unfold while they sat themselves, ordered drinks, and toasted each other. I ordered my second appetizer, as my meal, and feigned surprise when beer number three arrived right on schedule. The waiter and I exchanged a smile. My smile said, "Thank you." Whereas, I'm pretty sure his smile was saying, "How much can this girl drink?"

After a trip to view the glass case full of freshly baked desserts, I returned to my table to find my appetizer/

meal waiting. It was delicious. The portions were so incredulously small, I could have eaten two. I ate deliberately, savoring each bite. I was determined to prolong dinner, so I wasn't in and out in less than thirty minutes.

The people at the long table were ordering their meals. It was secretly captivating, because each of them asked several questions about the ingredients of different items and requested substitutions. I felt sorry for the wait staff. Soon after, another round of drinks landed at their table. I sipped my beer and placed my cutlery neatly on my plate signifying I was done with my meal. My beer was still half-full.

About this time, I heard Pops exclaim, "Is that girl *alone*?" God bless the elderly and their kid-like observations and lack of social filter.

A series of shhhh-es and, "yes, it appears so-s" came from the neighboring table.

And Pops said, "Not on my watch" and called out to me, "Hello, Miss??"

I pretended to be so engrossed in my empty, uncollected dinner plate that I didn't turn my head.

"Miss?" This time it was much louder and I had no choice but to turn and face him.

"Are you *alone*?" Pops asked incredulously.

I smiled, "I am, but it's OK. I just finished," holding my near-empty beer glass in salute.

"You must join us!" exclaimed Pops.

"That's OK," I said, now wondering why I had come to dinner at all. "You're just ordering, and I just finished."

"Nonsense," said Pops, and before I could even form another sentence, I saw a chair being added to the middle of their table and a fresh beer being brought on a tray and placed at the empty seat.

Well, I figured it would be rude not to join them after all that. But I did feel bad for the rest of them, having me thrust upon them, and wondered if Pops did this often.

As soon as I sat down, the introductions ensued. I learned who was related to whom and how this trip was courtesy of Pops for his eightieth birthday. We all chatted about our trip thus far, which led to sharing our plans for New Year's Eve and where else we had traveled.

At some point I excused myself and went to the restroom. By the time I'd returned, there was another full beer at my seat. As I sipped my beer, they passed some plates my way. I accepted a bit of food under the duress of "try this!" I held my stomach and groaned when a hot-fudge-something, complete with a sparkler, was put in front of every table guest, including me. I took two bites and imbibed in beer number five.

I thoroughly enjoyed that evening, meeting Pops' crew and learning of their adventures. And it was great to call out to them by name whenever I saw them for the rest of my stay. They insisted I was part of the family and, as such, I was to say, "I was traveling with family" when asked.

After saying goodnight to Pops and his crew, I went to the piano bar and spent some time with Jim-from-the-swim-ladder and his friend, Pete, and all the friends they'd made at the resort. We swapped stories about the menus and portion sizes. I gave a high-level overview of my new family and downplayed the eating-alone portion of the evening. Pete and Jim seemingly clung to my every word, both leaning in to hear me talking over the piano din.

"Have you tried the raspberry slide?" Pete asked and gestured toward the bar where a row of fruity drinks was lining the bar.

Jim turned and grabbed two, handing the second glass to me. Pete joined us a few minutes later, after grabbing one for himself and talking briefly to another woman standing nearby.

"I feel underdressed," Jim said in my ear. "You look so glamorous."

"Thank you. It feels good to dress up." I smiled, blushing.

Pete, who came across as less refined and seemed to craft conversation to create a one-man comedy routine, commented when he joined us: "Great dress. Shame you didn't wear it the other way around."

Laughing, Jim and I sipped our drinks. Our eyes met and held for a second or two longer than I expected. The glass was freezing in my hand, but I didn't want to break the moment by setting it down.

As the three of us stood together, drinks in hand, Pete motioned for the pianist to join our conversation. Talking was easier with her on break and the singer quietly fanning herself near the window. We learned that Pete and Jim met two years ago, when Pete joined the engineering firm where Jim had started working after college. Trying to appear closer to their age, I skirted questions about college and my current job, giving vague answers that omitted years or how much time had passed since college. If anyone caught on, they made no mention of it.

Jim and Pete could not have been more different in appearance. Jim was tall with dark blond, neatly styled hair. He wore jeans and a collared shirt. Pete, on the other hand, was in board shorts with disheveled, dark hair that gave the distinct impression he hadn't showered since that day's activities. Jim often started a conversation, only to have Pete derail it when his jokes landed and the group broke up in laughter, often at Jim's expense. Yet both of them seemed content with the dynamic, creating an easygoing banter between them.

Although Pete was directing his attention to the other woman in our group, I picked up something from him. He made lots of eye contact with me during his stories and would touch the small of my bare back, whenever he passed behind me on his way to the bar.

The group talked about New Year's Eve, which was the following night. The woman and I each described our plans, both different. Jim and Pete were still undecided on where they would go. I figured, especially at their age, they wanted to weigh all their options and make a decision at the last possible minute.

I was starting to regret my choice in shoes. The heels were killing my feet, and I needed to sit. I motioned to the group that I was moving to the nearby couch. Jim followed me. Contrary to Pete, Jim, having showered earlier, smelled faintly of the hotel's soap and kept the conversation going, seeming to have genuine interest in my answers. We talked for ages, with breaks as we went to the bar or restroom. I was really enjoying my time with him and was hoping it was leading somewhere. Shortly before midnight, with most of the crowed leaving the now-quiet bar, Pete walked over to say goodnight, motioning to the woman from earlier and smiling. We waved to her as Pete walked over to join her at the door.

An involuntary yawn escaped me and Jim, misunderstanding my action, said, "It's late. Let's catch up again tomorrow."

I thought maybe I had misread his attention during the snorkel trip or the spark I'd thought was mutual, as evidenced by his attentiveness at the bar, but I kept from seeming disappointed and simply said, "Absolutely, look for me on the beach."

8

There are two days in the year when I must be having fun: my birthday and New Year's Eve. I'm not talking about a dinner or movie or game night with friends. No, on these days, it's usually a trip somewhere exotic or a bucket-list item. Sometimes it works out, other times not so much.

With New Year's Eve upon me, I was eager to get the party started. The first day I'd arrived at the resort, I signed up for the trip to a street festival. The flyer promised food vendors, beer carts, and midnight fireworks—all the requisite ingredients for fun.

I knew I had to pace myself, since there would be more festivities that evening. I had devoured some fresh fruit, drunk a few tumblers of water, and floated in the ocean for about an hour. By late morning, I'd ended up at the pool.

Chatting with others in the pool, swimming sporadically, and getting out only when necessary, it was not surprising that time sped by. After applying a generous amount of sunscreen, I waded over to the bar for my first of many beers. At one point, some of us became so inspired by a song playing on someone's wireless speakers that we climbed from our barstools onto the poolside bar, creating a makeshift conga line.

Immediately, the bartender yelled, "No, no, no!" and we started to get down. To our collective surprise, however, he returned with some towels to lay out on the bar to prevent us from slipping and then waved us back up!

Our impromptu dance party was met with catcalls and cheers from the pool crowd. Really though, we did more laughing than dancing. After a couple of encores, we resumed our spots by the pool. By that time it was around 4:00. It was then that a couple from New York, who had been part of my dance troupe, asked me if I wanted to "join" them in their room before dinner. Even in my beer-filled state, I knew their invitation meant sex.

While I had plans to catch the bus to the street party at 10:00, I was intrigued, so I got their room number and met up with them a few hours later.

But, as fate would have it, the wife was very inebriated and had passed out on one of the beds in their room. I felt foolish arriving in my glittery gown, ready for my New Year's street party, while the husband answered the door in a towel, fresh from the shower. Looking in, I noticed the wife was under the covers, in a drunken slumber.

His partial nudity didn't faze me. I mean, we all had spent the past few days exclusively in our bathing suits. He invited me in and handed me a cold beer from the room's bar fridge. Then he gestured to the empty bed, suggesting I sit down. He excused himself, saying he was going to throw on some shorts and would return in a minute. It felt like I was in a scene in a porn movie. I half-expected corny music to start playing and for him to emerge from the bathroom, without shorts or towel, and then the scene would cut to us in a passionate embrace.

But he came out of the bathroom in shorts. We talked, somewhat awkwardly, for a few minutes. Then I set my beer down on the dresser by the door. I grabbed the room's door handle and turned to him. I didn't have a poignant line ready. In fact I had no real words. The menu had changed, and the special was no longer available. And it was obvious that neither of us were interested any longer.

He nodded as I opened the door.

I managed a "Safe travels," since I knew they were leaving the next afternoon.

And he said, "It was great meeting you."

I wish I could say we changed our minds or she woke up. Instead, I walked back to the piano bar and had a glass of champagne in hand, most likely before he'd even settled into bed.

9

Standing in the resort lobby in a dress so sparkly that it competed with the New Year's Eve decorations, I waited for the shuttle to take me to the street festival. Boasted as being an all-night event, it lived up to the hype. There was a collection of street vendors. Some had food carts, some sold beverages, and others displayed assorted craft items for sale. There were even some performers juggling bowling pins and twirling fiery batons. Walking around, I discovered a huge dance area, a stage, and a DJ playing current hits.

Did I mention that Jim was on the shuttle bus? With Pete?

It seemed their plans went from undecided to street festival, and I was thrilled to see them. I was also pleased to see Jim's mouth open at the sight of me in my dress and heels. They were both in shorts and nicely pressed shirts. I knew I was overdressed, but I was tanned and giddy, excited about the evening ahead.

Shortly after our arrival in town, there was a countdown to midnight. Apparently, we were celebrating the turn of the year in each time zone. Being a tourist destination, the town was doing it up well, making an effort to represent everyone's home that might be in attendance. We laughed and yelled with the crowd, screaming the countdown as the DJ said it.

At this first midnight, Jim and I kissed. It wasn't awkward, as might be expected with Pete looking on. It was gentle and soft, as if he were afraid somehow that he was going to injure me with his lips. The mutual attraction was real. It was apparent I hadn't misread any signals. When the kiss was over, he squeezed my hand briefly looking me straight in the eye, and we drew apart as we turned to walk on the uneven pathway.

The three of us wandered through the vendors after that, the guys eating indiscernible items from the different stations. I nibbled off their plates and grabbed us some beers from a man that was wheeling by on a bicycle, pushing an old-fashioned ice-cream cart. Everything was super cheap. Three cans of beer for three bucks.

And when the second midnight came around, Jim and I kissed again. We were definitely getting better at this! This time our lips met quicker, without hesitation and held together longer without parting. I felt his arm around my waist pulling me closer and his other hand started to gently stroke my hair. It was hard to believe we could be sharing this private moment in the middle of a bustling street party, less than ten feet from his friend.

Less than an hour from our current time zone celebration, we navigated to the dance floor and the three of us danced, jostling one another as the crowds pushed in and out of the area. We kept saying to each other, "This is so much fun!" And it was. And even better that all three of us thought so. Occasionally, one of us would negotiate our way out of the dance pit to get a few more cans of beer, usually saying "stay here" to the others as we left. With the sizable crowd, it was a small miracle that we found our way back.

At the real countdown to midnight, just before 3-2-1 was called, I leaned in purposefully to kiss Pete on the cheek. I didn't want him to feel that I'd taken Jim from him on their trip together and ruined his New Year's, and I also didn't want him to just stand there awkwardly while Jim and I participated in kiss number three. But he strategically turned his head and our lips met. When the countdown ran out, we were still kissing.

I was worried Jim might be upset. But he was laughing and teased, "Trying to steal my girl?"

Pete stepped back: "Happy New Year, man!" and the men exchanged a drunken hug.

Post-kiss, our trio carried on as it had. More dancing, more beer, another couple of countdowns, and me finally taking off my heels and riskily walking barefoot. It was past two in the morning when Jim, Pete, and I returned to the resort. No sooner had we stepped off the shuttle, when I ran into one of the members of my "family" that I had met at the dinner earlier that week.

"Rebekah! Happy New Year!"

An unsteady, sweaty arm wrapped around my neck.

The woman, one of Pop's daughters, said to me, "I'm looking for champagne" and pointed to the tub of ice and various drinks that were available on the front lawn of the resort that had earlier served as a celebration area. We managed to find an unopened bottle, and she said the rest of the family was in the resort's disco.

I turned to Jim and Pete, "Hey, my family's in the disco. You interested in going?"

I answered their puzzled looks with, "I met them at dinner the other night. They're a fun group. I joined them, and they told me I was part of the family now."

Jim and Pete nodded and we headed toward the disco. The scene was loud, smoky, and cold. At one point, Jim walked over to me and slipped his hand into mine. "You ready to go?" he semi-shouted in my ear.

I nodded and waved goodbye to my "family," but I couldn't find Pete.

"Is Pete staying?"

Jim shook his head, and we walked along the path from the club and headed in the direction of my room. And then Pete appeared and took my other hand, smiling. I looked at Jim and then at Pete.

Suddenly, I realized what had almost happened earlier in the evening with the couple from New York was about to happen with my countdown partners.

I didn't ask questions. I didn't state the obvious. There were no subtitles needed. I understood, and I was all in.

Pete gently opened the door to my room and Jim hung the "do not disturb" sign on the doorknob before closing the door behind him.

And guy number forty, guy number forty-one, and I counted down to midnight. Again.

10

THE BARTENDER

That trip to the Dominican, the day after the surreal New Year's Eve encounter with Jim and Pete, taught me an important lesson. It was New Year's Day, and I went on a scuba trip in the pristine sea. Despite the pain in my head and my intense sense of thirst, I knew the sea would cure my ailments.

I managed, without much effort, to have the divemaster set up my equipment and feed me an orange as we traveled to the first site. I confided my hungover status to him—a big no-no in the scuba world. He simply nodded and took me on as his pet project.

Between dives, instead of tending to my equipment, swapping out my empty oxygen tank for a full one, and updating my logbook, I floated on my back in my inflated vest, letting the waves carry me as I rocked back and forth near the boat's ladder. It was heavenly, but it earned me the nickname of "princesa," the Spanish word for "princess," by the divemaster. Despite being mocked, I enjoyed the five-star service and figured my new moniker was a small price to pay for milking a hang-over.

I'd regained my mojo before we reached the last dive site. The divemaster brought my equipment to me in the water and fitted on my vest without me even having to participate. I pictured that this must be like how they do it in the movies, when the actor doesn't know how to scuba dive, so the crew does all the work.

Underwater, I reflected on the scenery and the bliss-ful solitude where all you could hear was your own breathing. I remember distinctly thinking "New Year's Day underwater, what could be better?"

After the final dive, we all boarded the boat and re-moved our gear. I moved to the bow to catch some sun on our ride back. Predictably, the divemaster, who'd been my personal butler for the day, made his way to the bow, suddenly without any tasks, and took a seat beside me. We engaged in the usual travel dialogue about where was I from, how long I'd been diving, and why I traveled alone.

Men in all countries are inherently fascinated by a woman traveling alone. It was not lost on me that he hoped I would meet up with him at a local club he was going to with the crew. My engagement in the conversa-tion likely led him to believe it was going to happen, but I knew that was not even on my radar. I was leaving the country in a couple of days and had every intention of attending the resort's beach party that night. Despite my earlier state, I had rebounded and was once again ready to live it up Dominican-style. So, the divemaster was going to have to settle for a good tip, instead of a good time.

Back at the resort with a nap and dinner behind me, I ran into some familiar faces in the piano lounge. We talked about our adventures and drank complimentary champagne. I was wearing a white dress that enhanced my tan. And it wasn't just a simple sundress: It was an above-the-knee linen dress that I had bought in Europe while visiting a friend. The underlayer hugged my curves, and the top layer gave the look of antique lace. My blond hair, lightened by the sun, was loose and fell in layers around my face. My hair was fuller than usual due to the humidity, and I wore no makeup other than subtle pink lip gloss.

Later in the evening I received an "award" from the resort for winning poolside bingo at their nightly entertainment showcase. It was a small trophy with the words "Bingo Champion" written on the front. Jokingly, other guests asked me to pose for photos holding my award, and I did my best Angelina Jolie, appearing gracious while flirting with my "fans."

Everyone was in good spirits that evening. The assembled group of resort guests had various departure dates—all having arrived on different flights from various cities. I was thankful that Sophia, whom I'd met earlier in the trip, had also been eager to go to the beach party.

The unattached men in the group, numbers forty and forty-one included, were noncommittal about the trek down the boardwalk to the area where lights were strung up on posts. So, Sophia and I set off on our own toward the beach. The boardwalk slats, however, presented a problem for my stilettos. So, I quickly took them off and carried them in my right hand, while nursing a half-drunk flute of champagne in my left hand.

Although the boardwalk trip took mere minutes by day, we strolled leisurely and took ridiculous pictures of each other pretending to pose like runway models. Sophia, who had a keen sense of humor, kept walking up and then back as if it were a catwalk, flipping her hair and swishing her hips with each turn. I had to set my champagne glass down to take pictures and eventually lost track of it. That's the beauty of all-inclusive resorts. Wasting alcohol is never frowned upon, since there's always more where that came from.

Arriving at the beach party, we saddled up to the bar that was just a few feet from the makeshift area where an outdoor feast was winding down. Under the lights we could see the resort had created a dance floor and an additional bar on the beach. Music was blaring from giant speakers that were facing the sea. Sophia and I, still laughing at our brief modeling careers, joked about how the makeshift bar was less than fifty feet from the regular bar, at the edge of the sand. We spoke in whimsical British accents about how relieved we were that they had a second bar for those who might have trouble making it to the regular bar. Fortunately, the music drowned us out, so others did not have to listen to our bad accents or tipsy musings.

We decided we'd hit the dance floor as soon as a good song came on. After all, there was no point losing our great seats for a bad song. Sophia spoke a bit of Spanish and kept striking up conversations with the staff, leaving me wondering what they were discussing. Afterward, she usually disclosed that she told them crazy things about me—like how I was looking for my poodle on the beach or that I was really a man. All of it was in good fun, no matter how little sense it made to either of us.

The bartender was something out of a magazine with well-developed biceps that made his white mono-grammed resort golf shirt cling to him like a second skin. Native to the Dominican Republic, he was either nat-urally dark or perpetually tanned. And surprisingly for a resort, he didn't speak any English other than drink names. I had never seen him working before, but I had never ventured to the beach after dark during my stay.

Sophia and I continued our inappropriate joking, say-ing how we would like to pack him in our luggage and take him home as a souvenir. We quipped that he should have been on the brochure, and the resort would have sold more trips. Sophia continued to speak with him in Spanish. While I didn't know Spanish, I knew it was more words than just a drink order. She wouldn't tell me what she said; however, he looked at me during one of their conversations and went to fetch a champagne bottle. He filled a glass, set it in front of me and set a frozen bright red drink in front of Sophia. He blew a kiss at me and then left to serve other guests. All she would tell me was that she said that champagne was the best way to get to know me. We both laughed and then started to sing along with the music.

Sophia excused herself after the next round of drinks to venture to the restroom. I offered to accompany her, and she said, "No, stay with the hot dude. Keep him warm 'til I get back." While she was gone, a different drink was put in front of me. Something frozen and fruity and blue. The bartender gave me the thumbs-up and smiled a big, wide smile. I took a sip. And then another.

***

I woke up the next morning in my bed, nude. The air conditioning was off, and I was literally stuck to the sheets of my bed. I surveyed the room. Something wasn't right. Lots of things weren't right.

First off, what happened last night?

My dress, my beloved purchase, was in a pile right inside the front door. That was not like me. Even after a good party, my clothes would find their way to the back of a chair or a hook in the bathroom. Also, my room key was in bed with me. I found it when I rolled over. But it belonged in the slot by the front door, which was how the air conditioning functioned in resorts in the Caribbean.

Why would I not have put it there?

And where are my shoes?

While trying to piece it all together, I realized I didn't have a hangover. Nothing like the previous day where I'd struggled at sea. Today my head felt fine, but I just couldn't remember a damn thing. And my ribs hurt.

Why did my ribs hurt? Maybe from all the laughing?

A shower would help. I'd never had a blackout episode of any sort. *I mean, geez, had it come to this? Did I really drink that much?* After the shower, with a towel wrapped around me, I retrieved my crumpled dress and placed it over the arm of the sofa. The hem was ripped, or at least part of it was. And part of the antique lace had pulled away from the underlayer. And it had a red stain on it. *Had someone spilled wine on me?* That's when I noticed grass stains on the front of my dress. I sat on the sofa and quickly stood. My backside stung.

Had I fallen?

I walked toward the bed to get the room key to start up the AC. That's when I saw the blood on the sheets.

11

It was my last full day at the resort. After showering and using the toilet I realized nothing on me was bleeding, not anymore at least. I dressed in a bikini with a sundress overtop and packed my beach bag of usual necessities and headed to the pool. No breakfast for me. Besides, it was 11:30 a.m. The restaurant was likely closed.

I poured a fruit juice from the self-serve station and set my bag near a poolside chair in the shade. I sprayed on some SPF 30 and spread a towel over the lounger. The pool was already busy. My mouth was a desert. I gulped my fruit juice. Then I downed another glass. And after that, I dug in my bag and guzzled a bottle of water.

Despite my shady spot, I felt hot. I slipped into the pool, keeping my sunglasses on. Normally I removed them, ever vigilant to guard against a sunglass tan. But today was not normal. Today I didn't care about my tan or my champagne glass or where the rest of the guests I knew were. Today I needed solitude.

Around 3:00 p.m., the usual suspects gathered at the pool chairs and tables for daily bingo. Just a day ago, I was elated at my win at the pool party. Today I didn't care. Today I stayed in the pool. And that's when I saw Sophia. She glanced at the pool and I thought she saw me. I waved and then dropped my arm when I saw she didn't respond. I got out and looped my towel around my chest and walked toward her.

"Hey!" I said.

She said, "Have fun last night?" and I involuntarily giggled.

"What happened to you?" I asked.

"*Me*?" she responded. "You were gone when I got back from the bathroom. And so was the hot bartender. Couldn't even wait to tell me you were leaving? Some girl was serving drinks when I got back. I waited for a while. I mean your shoes were still there under your barstool, so I figured you were on the dance floor. I left about a half hour later."

"Oh, sorry," was I all I could muster.

"You should stay in the shade for a bit, you are getting a weird sunburn on the back of your neck" were the last words she said to me. I nodded and went to my beach chair to throw on my sundress.

Not long after, while in the restroom by the pool, I saw that the sunburn Sophia had seen on my neck wasn't a sunburn at all. It was four red stripes. They were in the shape of fingers. Fingers that had marked my skin as they had grabbed my neck. A more thorough inspection in the full-length mirror in my room showed a clear, red outline of a handprint on my ass cheek, too.

And as far as my ribs were concerned, they still hurt.

I laid low, skipped dinner, and went to the piano bar around 8:00 that evening. The guests were in full sing-a-long mode. A few recognized me and came over, eager to celebrate what was the last night for some of us. Number forty-one was there. He raised his glass in a salute of hello. I nodded and managed a smile in response. A server, as if conditioned to respond to my entrance, handed me a glass of champagne. I don't think I even finished a full sip before I set it down. I was feeling better, but still uncertain and a little taken aback that I was suddenly having drinking blackouts. It was not long before I tucked myself into bed with the alarm set for my departure back home the next day.

I flew home on January 3 and that night I drove myself to a nearby hospital. I told the intake nurse that my ribs were hurting and causing me shortness of breath. She asked very pointed questions on how it happened. My responses of "I don't know" were not received well.

"I won't get you in to see a doctor until you tell me what happened. Is someone hurting you?"

I was tempted to make up a story about a sports injury but finally confessed to the lost time two nights before.

I was suddenly fast-tracked—although I will admit the waiting room was quiet at that hour—I was whisked to a room, alone, with posters on the wall about safe needle exchanges and suicide hotlines. But then I sat in that room, alone, for two hours before someone returned. I repeated the whole story, the little bits I knew, to yet another person. She left and returned with her nursing supervisor, and I was asked to recount the details once again.

The nursing supervisor talked to the other nurse like I wasn't even in the room. She advised the nurse to schedule me a chest X-ray and to complete a pelvic exam.

Wait...what?

I protested and stressed that it was my ribs that hurt, not anything else. However, she continued talking to the nurse as if I weren't there. And then, again, I was alone in the little room. This time I was reading the fine print of the needle exchange posters, noting they were printed in Michigan and distributed by "Finer Prints." The irony was not lost on me.

Another hour passed.

The nurse, without her supervisor, returned. She told me she was taking me for my chest X-ray and would collect me when I was done. After the X-ray she walked me back to the main reception area and told me that I needed to wait for the results. Surprisingly, my name was called several minutes later, and I approached the desk where I had initially checked in. A different intake clerk was there and escorted me to a small desk with high partitions a short distance from the waiting area. My small-room nurse returned and upon determining I had no medication allergies handed me a bottle containing twelve tablets of Percocet, a strong and highly addictive pain killer, bearing my name.

She said I had bruised ribs, likely from direct contact with a blunt, solid surface. She told me that she would not perform the pelvic exam, due to my protests, but strongly encouraged me to visit the Rape Crisis Center at another hospital about half an hour away. I wouldn't have bothered, except now I was wanting a test for sexually transmitted diseases, something the first hospital did not offer.

Exhausted, I drove to the other hospital, as the sun began to rise. The wait commenced again. Another room, alone.

This time the room had instruments in a drawer, which, if someone had been in a truly devastated state, could have caused great self-injury. I was making a mental list of recommendations for these hospitals on how to handle cases like mine. Nothing like someone presenting with indicators of rape and being left alone in a room for hours with sharp instruments and a fresh bottle of Percocet.

The need for a pelvic exam and swabbing resurfaced. Many times. Once I made it perfectly clear that I had no intention of pressing any charges, they agreed the kit would be a waste of time. After I had blood drawn, I gave a urine sample, took the morning-after pill, and agreed to a cursory examination. I refused photographs, measuring of wounds, and counseling services. The pregnancy test was negative but needed to be repeated in a week.

My urine also came back positive for a list of drugs I had never heard of. She said they were often slipped in a woman's drink to incapacitate her and can take effect in as little as fifteen minutes.

Fifteen minutes?

That was probably the amount of time Sophia was in the washroom. And enough time for me to down the mysterious blue drink while I was alone. Good Lord.

They told me I needed a pregnancy test the following week and tests for HIV in the coming months. I was also instructed to avoid unprotected sex until the results were known. My head was spinning from all the instructions. And then I knew what I would save the bottle of Percocet for. If I tested positive for HIV, that whole bottle was going in me. For sure.

I was repeatedly encouraged to accept counseling. Instead, I chose that moment to verbally itemize, quite calmly, the way this system had failed me. Then I said they'd best mend their practice before another victim came through the door.

I told them I didn't need counseling, because I didn't remember anything.

And just when I thought I was getting off easy, the nurse countered with, "You don't remember now. But you will. The memories come back."

Months later, with all the HIV and pregnancy tests having negative results, I threw the bottle of Percocet in the garbage. I had never even opened it, bruised ribs and all. And that nurse was right, I did remember. Not all in a flash, but a bit over time. I remember hands on my neck and two or three different male voices speaking Spanish to each other. I remember being bent forward over a concrete bench in a flower garden and one, perhaps two men, taking turns from behind me. In my memories, I could tell it was still resort property from the manicured lawns, but a place I had not seen. And I remember indiscernible words being whispered in my ear in broken English.

I don't remember their faces or how I returned to my room and thankfully I don't remember much else. I don't even think about it anymore. I cried after that first night in the hospital and right before each HIV test. And I only told one person—a close female friend I knew wouldn't say "that's what you get for traveling alone."

Oddly enough, I might have consented to the bartender, if given the opportunity. That was what caused me the most confusion and uncertainty. He didn't give me that option.

Months later, I finally put the episode behind me and compartmentalized it. And, in case you're wondering, the bartender(s) don't get a number. They aren't on my list. They don't deserve it.

12

NUMBER THIRTY-FIVE

I married guy number thirty-five.

We had met at the bank—the same place I worked when I met guy number thirty-three, but from a completely different department.

Ben did the exact same job as me: same desk, same case files, same pens. He worked the day shift and at 4:00 p.m. he handed his work off to me. Then I took over until 11:00 p.m. Fraud doesn't sleep, so that is why I was lucky enough to find such a great-paying job that suited my schedule.

During the work transition each weekday, he would share funny anecdotes of clients he'd dealt with or leave me notes on the paperwork, describing the painfully long phone call it took to manage a particular case. I was drawn to his humor. I, too, began leaving notes of the woes of my work night or other such nonsense. Anecdotes eventually turned into more thoughtful exchanges like, "I found this CD you might like," or "There's a cupcake in the fridge for you, leftover from the staff birthday party today." We both participated in the notes, the exchanges, and the flirting.

Although, he went to Calvin's most nights as part of our assimilated group over the years, we had never previously met, not even when I was dating guy number thirty-three. Not until we shared a workstation did our paths cross. On occasion, the departmental director would breeze through our mostly vacated floor, usually around 7:00 p.m., and tell me and my coworkers to go for an extended break. I had discovered this director made this generous gesture due to his state of inebriation as well his obvious crush on my female boss. The extended break for me and the other staff would give them some extra time alone. I always pounced on this opportunity and made my way to Calvin's, knowing I was immune to any repercussions, given the looks and subtle touches I had seen pass between the two of them over the preceding months. They were married, but not to each other. I was twenty-three years old and already figuring out how to make situations work in my favor.

On such occasions I made my way back to work around 9:00 p.m., with enough time to finish up my essential tasks for the day or to fake it until my shift ended, depending on my sobriety. On one particular night, Ben was still at the bar when I arrived.

"What are you doing here at seven?" he asked.

"Same thing as you," I replied.

"Are you finished with work already?"

It turns out he was considerably more straitlaced than me and the thought of me consuming alcohol mid-shift made him recoil in horror. I mostly ignored him that night, determined not to ruin my good time with unnecessary guilt.

Ben and I bumped into each other socially about a month after that, at a coworker's going-away party. I had changed my shift to end earlier, as the guest of honor was a good friend. By the time I made it to the bar around 8:00 p.m., the party was well underway.

The revelry lasted until the bar closed at 1:30 a.m. The bank paid everyone's check, cementing the reason in my mind why bank fees were so high. Ben was unable to drive and was going to catch a ride with a sober colleague.

While I was giving my departing friend a long hug with the usual promises to stay in touch, Ben approached me, drunkenly, and asked, "How are you getting home?" Before I could respond, he then said it to others, or no one really, pointing to me, "How is she getting home?"

I responded that I was taking the subway, catching the last one, in fact, and had to run. I heard him yell, "Hey, wait!" as I sprinted across the street toward the station. I didn't even slow my run. At that time, the subway seemed more important than Ben.

Not long after, perhaps a few weeks later, while reviewing the paperwork on my desk, I came across a note in the mix that said, "Have dinner with me?" I was immediately aware that the note was in the form of a question, instead of something more forceful like, "Have dinner with me!"

I left my response via sticky note, in the same spot of his/my/our desk, saying, "OK, where?"

***

Ben and I moved in together after a year of dating. My basement apartment was barely big enough for one person, let alone two, so, after a few months of cramped living quarters we relocated to a suitable, slightly larger apartment in the downtown core, a mere subway station away from my current residence.

It was official. We were a couple. We signed the lease together, and both families helped with the move. We had the customary housewarming parties and overnight guests. We hosted rudimentary dinners and attended weekend luncheons with parents. We explored the city together. We bought secondhand furniture and ate whatever groceries we could afford. Soon after moving in together, I left the job at the bank for a job at the lake's marina, where I could be outside. In true do-now-think-later fashion, I gave up security and financial windfall for adventure. The bank paid three times what I made at my new job. While perhaps not the wisest decision, it would not be the last time in my life I would choose happiness over security.

Ben was very supportive of my decision to work at the marina. My new job afforded me a chance to work on the water, which I loved, and it gave me a new batch of friends and a new hangout after work. And most importantly, a world separate from the one I was part of once I got home.

I'm not sure when I realized I'd made a mistake moving in with Ben.

I knew consciously, in the moment, that I regularly pushed the boundaries of our relationship. Seizing on the fact that he was so grateful to have me in his life, he questioned so little of what I did. I didn't cheat, but I did build a world that did not include him, which I guess is an indirect way of cheating, since I was creating this whole separate life, in case the one I had with him didn't work out. And, strangely, I was happy that he never came to my work, never met my work friends, didn't hang out with us at the lakeside bars after shift, or come to the day trips on my coworker's boat on our days off.

I liked living two lives.

Our circumstances later took Ben and me out of downtown and into the suburbs. We had graduated to a two-car life with a condo overlooking a wooded ravine. While beautiful, this was a world I'd never imagined for myself. We were in the town Ben had grown up in. This was his home turf. If there was one thing I could do for him, it was afford him a life where he could regularly see his parents, his siblings, and continue his childhood friendships.

I, unfortunately, was a fish out of water. I missed the city, the friends that I no longer saw regularly, and the general independence life had given me. In spite of that,

I loved our home and helped with the decorating, painting, maintenance, and entertaining. We frequented the wing joint in the lobby of our seventeen-floor building, and our condo was a regular hot spot for our friends to hang out. It was a happy time. In a word, we were content.

But, what I knew, and Ben didn't, was this was not a normal relationship. Having had a series of boyfriends since high school, including a serious relationship, I knew there was something missing. We were missing the attraction and the physical closeness. And the sex.

After about a year of living in the new condo, our friends started getting engaged. Like us, many of them already lived together, but now they were sealing the deal. For one wedding we traveled to Wales, bound for the small hometown of the bride that Ben's best friend had met during law school abroad.

Nothing tested a relationship more than travel, especially for those as unaccustomed to it as Ben was. We finally made it to the wedding destination, ensuing some crazy hiccups along the way, including hilarious eruptions of laughter that had us both sitting on our luggage, breathless, on a barren street just blocks from the train station in a remote Welsh town.

Before arriving in Wales, our so-called European tour included stops in Belgium and London. We stopped in Belgium because Ben's uber-annoying brother and uber-snobby sister-in-law lived there. It was a temporary, two-year assignment for them. Their real home was in

Arizona. We visited during the second year of their stay and saw their gorgeous home they got as part of his business relocation.

The day we arrived went unexpectedly well. Snobby got drunk and dropped the walls she regularly put up. I actually enjoyed her company that day—a day where she didn't have to point out how much money they had, where she didn't ask me where I bought my clothes or talk about designers I'd never heard of.

When Annoying got home from work, he was unimpressed with the state his wife was in. He was equally nonplussed that dinner was not ready, although the running joke in the family was the best thing she ever made were reservations.

Since they lived in the middle of nowhere, not far from the French border, ordering in was not an option. So, we ate cheese and crackers off a marble platter—fancy French cheeses and deluxe crackers with bits of fruit and nuts in them. My plate was made of gold-leafed china. The dishes were French, I was told.

"Oh, good. I like my plate to come from the same place as my cheese." I retorted.

Snobby laughed, for a change.

Annoying did not.

Our time with them was busy. We explored Belgium, including a ski lodge, which, in the summer, made for a great hiking hill with terrific views. It could have been great, were it not for Annoying, who kept making all these snide comments about how I was holding Ben back in life. Holding him back from what, I wasn't sure. The recurring theme seemed to be that I just wasn't good enough for Ben.

True to form, like a vegan that reminds you repeatedly of their dietary preference, the conversations with Annoying frequently turned to income and who made how much. Ben's brother was quick to say that quitting my job at the bank had been foolish. I didn't want to get into it with him, so I drank more to block out the noise.

Near the end of our stay, I modeled the dress I intended to wear to the upcoming wedding in Wales. It was the only dress I'd brought for that event and was quite excited at my choice. It was an elegant dress—a simple light green sheath with purple lilacs on it. The back hem was longer than the front. And my white strappy sandals completed the ensemble.

I thought maybe Snobby and I had bonded on this trip, if only over alcohol, but I couldn't have been more wrong. With the dress on, I stepped out of her walk-in closet—a room filled many mirrors.

"Funny girl. Now what dress are you really wearing?"

I stopped walking. My mouth opened, but I had no words to convey what I was feeling in that moment. Later on I realized I'd been simultaneously attacked, ridiculed, and humiliated.

Right then, Ben walked in the room and said, "Love that dress. You look great."

Then Snobby said, "Well, it's too late to buy something else. I suppose now you're stuck with it."

I looked over at Ben. Our eyes locked. He could see me fighting off a sea of emotions and once back in our room, I broke down in tears, letting the frustration of the entire visit out, right there in his arms.

13

During our visit to London, I took Ben to all my old haunts. I showed him where I worked that summer during college. We visited all the touristy spots and my ultimate favorite bar in Covent Garden. He was not as excited as I'd hoped he would be with my tour. He liked London, he just didn't *love* it, as I had and still did. It was not for a lack of trying on my part. I pulled out all the stops, taking him from one place to the next, desperate to get him to fall in love with the city as I had. But he didn't warm to it. I had to accept it wasn't his thing—London or traveling, really.

While we were there, we spent a drunken day in a bar off the beaten track. Despite it being a random Wednesday, it was summer, and it was packed with Londoners and tourists alike. There was even a live band and both European and North American sports played on various mounted televisions.

At some point, Ben and I lost track of one another. I think it was when I went to the restroom. Or when he did. This tends to happen when I go out. I like to mingle, introduce myself, and chat with a variety of people. Not in a pickup-line sort of way, but more in a live-every-moment-to-its-fullest manner. I would never leave the bar without him, but I also didn't feel the need to panic and track him down. Eventually I saw him sitting by himself, absorbed in an American football game that was playing on one of the screens.

Instead of sitting down next to him, I got to talking to a guy from London, and we hit it off.

We were standing at a tall table, without stools, that was formed around a pole that went from floor to ceiling. We talked about traveling, London, and what had brought us to the bar. At one point, Ben came over and joined the conversation. Although there really wasn't room for us all, a couple of girls joined the table, too. After awhile, Ben wandered back to a table near the bar to watch the game, and the girls and I waded into a deep discussion over British sitcoms, while the guy looked on, amused.

I excused myself to go to the restroom and returned to the table to find just the girls. I was surprised how disappointed I was that the mystery man was gone. I was turning to leave the girls and locate Ben, when the guy reappeared and took me by the hand and led me toward the band and the bar's dance floor. We danced four songs straight and headed to the bar for another beer. We passed Ben on the way. I asked him if he wanted to dance with us, already knowing the answer.

"No, you go ahead, I'm happy here with the game and my pint."

Last call was being announced. I couldn't believe it was midnight already. We'd been there eight hours! With a fresh beer in hand, the guy motioned with his head toward the dance floor again. Following, I saw he kept walking past the dance floor and headed for the restrooms. I must have misunderstood. I stopped near the restroom entrance and put my beer on a nearby table, deciding to use the facilities while I was in that corner of the bar. When I came out of my stall and was at the sink, I looked up in the mirror to find him behind me. I saw his reflection in the mirror. In the *women's* bathroom.

I was not alarmed. Nor was I was scared. Instead, I was excited. I spun around and threw my arms around his neck. He walked backward into a stall with me still wrapped around him. We made out with an intensity I had never experienced. It was like we knew we had limited time and had to fit all our attraction into just a few minutes.

We were catching our breath when I heard Ben's voice.

"Rebekah???" "Are you in here?" The bar is closing!"

He sounded pissed off. The guy had the good sense to jump on the back of the toilet so his feet would not show underneath the stall door. I answered Ben, trying to sound calm, like I wasn't out of breath from a cheap, but great, bathroom make-out session.

"Yep, just changing my tampon. Give me a minute, for God's sake."

My words came out sharper than intended. Ben likely sensed it was not normal. He came closer to the stall door. I looked back at the guy. He appeared very nervous, and his arms extended, ready to defend himself.

I couldn't just open the door with Ben standing so close. So I said, sternly, "Fine, go back to the bar. You can't be in here!"

I flushed the toilet for good measure and opened the stall door when I heard him retreat. And while I couldn't stop smiling, I didn't even turn around to say goodbye to the guy who had just blown my mind.

"Hurry up," Ben said. "They're trying to close the place up. We're the last ones here."

Except that we weren't.

14

The next day was uneventful. I wanted to go sight-seeing, but Ben wanted to stay in and watch TV in the cramped hotel room.

Irritated, I said things like, "How often are you in the British capital?" and "Is this really how you want to spend your time here?"

Finally, primarily out of guilt, I stayed with him that day. Continuing the ruse of being on my period, I hung out in the room with him until we decided on an early dinner at a pub nearby. The guilt was legitimate. Ben didn't do anything wrong, per se. He just didn't have that sizzle or desire for intimacy that I craved. It frustrated me. Often.

But our relationship also had its share of good times—times where I arrived home from work on a Friday evening to a home-cooked meal and candles glowing and our favorite band playing on the stereo. The wine would be chilled and there would be two crystal glasses on the table. He would take my coat, ask about my day, and bring me a serving spoon full of whatever sauce the chicken was cooking in. We would chat about whatever person was behaving crazy at our respective workplaces, and we would laugh.

There were also times that brought me to tears. But I kept that from him and did my crying in the shower. I think it was partly because I was embarrassed. I thought maybe there was something wrong with me. I mean, why couldn't I just be happy? Here I was with this great guy, yet my bouts of crying were becoming more frequent.

My frustration stemmed from his impenetrable tie to his family. He hadn't matured or distanced from his family as much as I had from mine, or our friends had from theirs. I had no issue with his frequent calls or visits to them. However, I did have an issue with the influence they extended over his life. And mine.

He checked with them for seemingly everything--from major decisions, such as whether to buy a car or change jobs, to minor decisions, like whether he should dry-clean his down coat and what type of cheese he should put in the casserole. He often canceled our plans, because his parents wanted to take him out for dinner or take him shopping for fall clothes or accompany them to visit a flea market.

One exceedingly crushing blow came when Ben came home excited from a Sunday family dinner, one where I had not been invited, and announced that we were all going to Florida on a family vacation.

"We are?? When?" I asked, joining his excitement.

He went on to give details. It was scheduled for Thanksgiving. In Tampa. All of us. It sounded great. His parents were affluent and no doubt the accommodation would reflect that.

It was about a week later that I learned that "all of us" did not include me. I was "welcome to come" but would have to pay my own way, something that was impossible even with our combined income.

I oscillated between being sad and being livid. Who does that? I mean, who invites an entire family, including in-laws and children and cousins and aunts, but insists one girlfriend pay her own way?

We didn't end up going.

I wasn't self-aware enough at the time to encourage Ben to go without me. I was too proud and felt we needed to take a stand, not-too-subtly suggesting to him that if he went, there would be hell to pay with me. I wish I could say that was the end of their manipulative ploys to end our relationship, but similar incidents occurred. Invites to dinners at fancy restaurants were conveniently arranged when my schedule didn't permit me to attend, and another time they belittled my outfit at a Christmas Eve dinner, where I had dressed in a festive taffeta dress, while the rest were in khakis and sweaters. That incident upset me to the point that I left, distraught, before dinner was served. Whereas, Ben—fearful of conflict, no matter the cost—stayed behind to appease his family.

Another particularly soul-sucking moment happened at a cabin Ben and I had rented for New Year's. The group included me and Ben, his parents, his sister and brother and their spouses. Snobby had found the cabin too cold and constantly complained about the snow; whereas, Annoying kept bragging about how he could have found a better cabin.

Ben's father, more than tipsy, was in rare judgmental form. Despite being a cohost, I felt like I was crashing a party I had not been invited to. The evening continued. Unfortunately, it went from bad to worse.

Finally, Ben's brother-in-law, Angelo, tried to change the subject by suggesting we play some board games or read current events from a magazine. His attempt at keeping the peace was short-lived. We brought in the new year with Annoying handing everyone $2,000 cash at the stroke of midnight. I declined mine. Frankly, I was offended. Offended of the overture after such disdain was shown to me. It was a shallow move for Annoying to show his power in the family that way.

Little did I know the group would swarm and insist I take the gift. "It's not like you're in any position to refuse," Ben's father chided.

When it was clear from the screaming match that rejecting the cash wasn't possible, I was pointedly instructed to spend it on our upcoming wedding, which was a mere eight months away. Realizing it was futile to refuse the manipulative gesture, I took it. However, instead of spending it on our wedding, I spent it on clothes and lunches with friends. The money was squandered within a week.

15

Shortly thereafter, I became reclusive at Ben's family events. I was not cooperative in assimilating, and Ben was unwilling to gain independence. We were at a crossroads. "Nothing solves a crossroads better than getting married," said no therapist ever.

A month before our wedding, a colleague at work had their own rehearsal dinner on a Thursday night, for a Saturday wedding. The reasoning was so the night before the wedding wouldn't be a drunken affair and the bride and groom could enjoy the entire Friday with their selected wedding party. I loved the idea and bounced it off Ben. He also thought it was great, and we set the plan in motion.

We also decided our wedding meal, the evening portion, would be kid-free. This decision was reached after great discussion between the two of us, but really, it was prompted by me. It wasn't that I didn't like kids or didn't adore the handful of nieces and nephews in our wedding party, all under the age of five. The decision was to allow the parents of those children to engage and participate in the meal without distraction. It was a tough pill to swallow for our families, but they respected our wishes. Or so I thought.

About two weeks prior to our wedding, Ben's father reminded us that a blessing was required before the reception meal. This was important to him. It wasn't at all important to me, but I respected his faith, so I agreed. We asked Ben's father to do it. To our surprise, he suggested it would be cute for Logan to say the grace.

Wait, what?

Logan, our eighteen-month-old nephew, was in charge of making it down the aisle at the outdoor wedding but wouldn't be in attendance at the yacht club reception. Ben reminded his dad of the kid-free plan and his dad said, "Well, I didn't think that meant family! Logan will be devastated if he can't attend!"

I wasn't a parent, nor did I pretend to be an expert on parenting, but I was confident that Logan could only be devastated by someone taking away his soother, or by feeding him mashed pears. I felt certain that his life would not be altered by skipping a wedding reception.

That was the night that Ben's father took Ben out for dinner and told him not to marry me.

16

Ben recounted the events later that evening, after I pulled it out of him. I mean like really pulled ... Ben didn't want to give it up.

After I heard this, I asked Ben, "What did you say?"

"What could I say? I said, 'Rebekah said no kids.'"

I was floored.

"Wow. Me? What happened to you, Ben? Weren't we in agreement about that?"

I finished pacing, took a deep breath and tried to collect myself. But another sucker punch was waiting to catch me while I was still down. That's when Ben told me his dad had offered him cash to skip out on the wedding.

"What? He said *what*?"

Ben shrugged. The amount was not shared with me, but I had a feeling it would have been enough for him to buy a small island.

A while back, I had been debating whether or not I should take Ben's last name, post nuptials. Secretly, I had decided I was taking his name, but I kept him guessing to keep it a surprise. I'd even bought him a door knocker for the front door of our home, as a wedding gift, inscribed with our joint last name.

But after hearing this I told Ben, "Well, you have a decision to make. You can allow Logan to come to the wedding and say grace at our reception while my family attends childless, or you can stand up to your father."

Eighteen-month-old Logan said grace at the wedding. I never forgave Ben for that. Ben never got the inscribed gift, and I never took his name.

The marriage lasted three months. (Not counting as a real marriage, to me). Regardless, Ben took the break-up poorly. Truth be told, I never should have married him. Screw the deposits on the DJ, family loyalty, and all the head counts for chicken or fish. I should have told him how I felt before the wedding. But I swept my feelings and pride neatly under the runner, as I walked down that aisle and married him.

So, it came as no surprise to me when I delicately announced shortly after Christmas that I was leaving that I saw a brand-new side of him. Vindictive, petty, and conniving, he fought me tooth and nail on custody of every material possession, right down to the wedding china. Annoying had coached him on what to ask for in the divorce, along with what buttons to push. He even went so far as to pay for Ben's lawyer.

And while I had written thank-you cards for items that lined Ben's cupboards, I vowed I would never, even during a breakup, treat someone with such disrespect. It was so gut-wrenching to see him cast such a dark shadow on our years together, making the end the focus.

Over a decade later, I heard through a mutual friend that Ben and his family had never forgiven me. Ben claimed I'd ruined his life. But, deep down, I've always felt that I saved him. Saved us both from years of being together but feeling so alone.

17

NUMBER TWO

Guy number two was my first love.

We were in high school together, a very large school with about 1,200 students across four grades. I was in my final year of school, and Trevor was just a semester behind me. He was wise beyond his years, something even I could recognize at the time. He was going to go places, for sure.

We didn't really know each other that well at school. We weren't in any of the same classes. In fact, I don't even remember how we first met. But I do recall our first kiss. We were at a party. The house was near the school, and I remember it had lots of rooms and a huge yard, with one of those long, winding tree-lined driveways. The music from the party, along with all the shouting and laughing, could be heard all the way to the street. There were probably forty kids there, although there were only ten or so that I would classify as friends of mine.

While there, I went out for some fresh air and wandered into the front yard and was sitting on the rolling hills of the front lawn, facing the street. I remember thinking it was really peaceful. There was no traffic, and it was just me on the lawn with my thoughts. Earlier that night, I'd broken up with my boyfriend of eighteen months, aka guy number one. He had refused to come with me that night and often referred to my life as "infantile and mundane."

It was a conversation we'd probably had a dozen times before. Each time, not really understanding a relationship or my role in one, I begged for forgiveness and accepted his silence that followed—a silence I encountered whenever I did something that displeased him. He was about four years older than me, and, in your teens, a four-year age difference was like an entire lifetime.

This time, the familiar argument surfaced while we were heading to the party. He started complaining about my friends, the party scene, my outfit, and my constant need to go out. After months of incessant complaining, he'd hit my last nerve. So, I pulled over at an intersection and said, "Get out."

It was completely matter of fact and calm. There was no drama. I didn't even raise my voice. I was so calm, in fact, he didn't even hear me at first and asked, "Why are we stopping?"

I repeated, "If you don't want to go with me, then please get out."

So, he stepped out of the car. We were about ten blocks from his home and a twenty-minute drive to the party. He later told me he thought I would drive around the block and come back and get him.

He was wrong.

I continued on to the party, collecting a friend on the way, and guy number one and I never dated again.

I had not seen guy number two at a party before. Or maybe it was more that I hadn't *noticed* him before. But that night, while I sat on the front lawn, pondering my newfound freedom, he approached me and asked if I wanted company. Seeing Trevor, I realized I did. *His* company.

We chatted amicably about school and teachers. Turned out he'd been in one of my classes but only for a few weeks until he rearranged his schedule. He said he worked at the mall and mentioned a few friends that he was with that night—people who weren't in my circle.

After a while we walked back inside to find our friends and refill our drinks. Then we went for a walk on the private cul-de-sac the house was situated on. It was surprisingly easy to talk to Trevor. On our walk, I told him about my breakup and how I was surprisingly relieved.

And I remember he said, "Oh, so you don't have a boyfriend?"

"No, not anymore."

And then he kissed me. It wasn't pushy or sloppy—just a gentle lift of my chin with his hand and a soft kiss on my closed lips. It was nice. And different from guy number one. Good different.

And immediately after he said, "Want to walk back to the party now?"

I looked up at him and smiled. He gently squeezed my hand, and we headed back inside, hand in hand. And just like that, I wasn't upset about guy number one anymore.

***

This was a time before cell phones, texting, or group chats. Since we didn't exchange phone numbers, there was no way for Trevor to reach me over the weekend. When I got to school on Monday I saw him standing outside my first-period class.

Grinning from ear to ear he asked, "I was wondering if you might want to grab dinner sometime?"

I had butterflies all morning and was relieved to see him after class. Trying to contain my elation, I nodded, and we made plans to meet up at the mall Friday night after his shift. But before I could ask for his number, he was gone again.

Unfortunately, guy number one called often that week. Whenever the phone rang at home, I would cringe. After the first call when he said he'd forgiven me for my childish behavior and for recklessly leaving him on a street corner, I started dodging his calls and ignoring his messages. I also varied my routine to avoid bumping into him. By the end of the week, his pride must have kicked in, because instead of pleading and issuing backhanded apologies, he unleashed his pain and said, "I'm glad we're through. Now I can date someone grown up."

Maybe it sounds cold, or like I hadn't cared about our relationship, but I wasn't hurt by those words. I was done being hurt. Instead, I was relieved and somewhat concerned for the next girl he would date. While I didn't realize it at the time, he was a textbook narcissist. All I knew was I was relieved to be rid of him.

18

The Friday night dinner with Trevor was a success, as were the many dates that followed. However, things became strained when Trevor left for college. While I had chosen to go to college close to home, Trevor opted for the ivy league school where his parents had met. So, instead of having constant access to one another, there was now a lengthy drive between us and the new life away from home that was unfolding for him. To his credit, he did come home a lot of weekends during his first year away, which helped. However, by the second year, the trips home became less frequent. And in our final year together, even with the best of intentions, we barely saw each other.

That's when I strayed.

Shelby, a friend from college I'd met not long after Trevor and I started dating, literally spent every waking moment with me while he was away at school. Weekdays and weekends we were either at each other's home or waiting for one of us to finish work so we could hang out. We studied together and were a staple at the campus pub and the dance clubs near our homes.

And with Trevor away, I started to push the boundaries of fidelity. Together with Shelby, I would dance in bars with other guys (harmless), let them buy me drinks (still pretty harmless), and, sometimes, I'd indulge in a kiss or two (enjoyable, but a little less harmless).

On one such evening, at the pub near my house, I was dancing seductively with a guy to the DJ's music on the tiny dance floor. It held a dozen people, max. Any more dancers than that and you'd start to bump into people. I'm not even sure it was a real dance floor. It was more of an area where the floor tile gave way to a bit of hardwood. But on Thursday nights, it was where we danced. We'd be out there until we were drenched with sweat and spilled beer.

On one night, my dancing partner and I were glued together, swaying, rather than dancing, to the beat of the music. And suddenly, as we were slow-dancing, there was Trevor's next-door-neighbor and childhood friend, Jamin. When I saw him I did a double-take but stayed glued to my dancing partner while Trevor's friend kept looking at me as if I'd been cheating on *him*. His face was a cross between a scowl and a grin. Not wanting to make a big deal, or appear guilty, I let the song finish before leaving the dance floor to say hi to him.

Jamin never asked who the guy was, and I didn't offer an explanation. There was nothing to explain really. The whole scenario was pretty obvious. I was out having fun, I'd been caught, and I wasn't going to feel bad about it. The next day, sober and reflective, I did wonder if this would make it back to Trevor, but Trevor never brought it up during the phone calls we had over the next month or two. So, it seemed I was in the clear.

In fact, when he came home for a weekend in January, everything was just as it always had been. Not long after that we were talking about Valentine's Day and whether he was coming home that weekend.

When he said he was planning to come home, I reminded him we should make reservations if we wanted to get a decent table. But when he said, "Let's just stay in," I began to wonder if Jamin had said something after all.

I decided not to overthink it. Maybe Trevor just wanted some alone-time without the restaurant lines and to just snuggle up with some pizza and watch movies. I wanted to spend some time together, so it didn't really matter one way or the other to me what we did. A few days after he'd gotten home, I went over to his house. His mom let me in and said he was downstairs watching TV. I descended the stairs like I had a million times over the past three years, my feet landing on familiar wear patterns in the rug. When I got to the bottom of the stairs, I found him taping up a cardboard box.

He didn't look at me. Instead, my "Whatcha up to?" was countered with a terse, "Let's sit."

I will give Trevor credit. He was composed and his breakup speech was good. Scripted good. Like a made-for-TV movie that makes you cry good. You know the ones that teach you a lesson and still leave you feeling uplifted when it's all over. He didn't give a reason for the breakup, and I didn't ask. My not asking likely spoke volumes. Maybe on some level I already knew. I just didn't want to believe it.

After his speech, I picked up the box and went home. The box was filled with all the stuff I'd given him over the years, along with some things of mine that had ended up in his home over time. I didn't open it for about three months. It just sat in the back of my closet until one day I felt ready. When I opened it, I found the Valentine's gift he had bought me, laid right on top. It was a set of dog tags on a chain with both our names on it. I have to say it hurt a little to see how considerate he'd been. He was a decent guy. One that I had taken for granted. The least I could have done was to have been upfront with him. And I don't blame Jamin. He didn't do anything wrong. It was good that Trevor had friends looking out for him.

I carried those dog tags in my pocket periodically over the next year. They were a reminder of happier times and the penalty of my mistake.

It turns out Trevor married a woman four years later that could easily have been my identical twin or my movie stand-in. Friends of mine that went to the wedding found the resemblance uncanny. Instead of feeling jealous or unsettled by the likeness, I took it as a compliment. In spite of my relationship fumble, I guess I had some redeeming qualities after all.

19

NUMBER THIRTY-SIX

Guy number thirty-six and I eloped. Both the relationship and the nuptials were quick off the heels of my divorce from guy number thirty-five. While my first marriage didn't really count, given it lasted only a matter of weeks, this union held up for seven years, at least on paper.

As people, we couldn't have been more different. Derrick was ten years my senior and had grown up in a small town with a large family, sharing a bedroom with three other siblings. I grew up in a big city, relied on the subway before I could drive, came from a small family, and was the only child living at home after my grown brother moved out when I was eight years old.

I was freshly single, after marriage number one ended, the disaster I refer to as my "expensive learning experience." Guy number thirty-six had divorced his third wife, five years prior. I was encumbered by a home, a car, and a few houseplants. Whereas, he lived in a basement apartment and had three grown children, each from a different wife who all lived in various parts of the country. Not one of his adult children maintained a solid relationship with him, and he had a young grandson he had never met.

In addition to these obvious red flags, I also ignored our gap in education and income—me with my master's degrees and he with his grade school education. I encouraged him to read and resisted every impulse to correct his grammar when he spoke and filled in any form that accompanied him home from the doctor or his job at the factory. I read him his mail and followed up on his appointments, scheduling his trips to the dentist or optician. I cooked all his meals or left him homemade dinners with detailed preparation instructions when I was away. I even taught him how to fill out a bank check when he sent money by mail and showed him the basics of email. And once I asked him why he was heating his coffee for fifty seconds in the microwave. Why not a whole minute? His response, "I only wanted half a minute," left me incredulous.

I overcompensated for the gaps in our lives. The more I tried, the less he did. Or so it seemed. Despite all of this, I was in love with him. I rationalized that his previous wives were fools, bitches, or too dumb to see what they had. I never met any of his family. His parents lived in a small town on the coast and had never set foot on a plane, nor had any intention to. He flew to see them a couple of times a year, returning looking like he had aged five years with each visit.

Early in our life as a couple, not long after buying our dream home, Derrick became distant and irritated. I chalked it up to the stress of home ownership and the added chores that cut into his "guy time." He complained that he missed his time with his friends and that he missed his freedom. So, I took on more responsibility in the home and afforded him more time in pool halls, shady bars, and racetracks. That's when he started sneaking money out of the joint account, which I discovered when the mortgage bounced.

Maybe that is when I should have left, but I didn't.

Instead, I confronted him about the money. Asked questions. Probed. But I never raised my voice. There were no fits of rage or silent treatments, and our sex life never faltered. I was very much the dutiful wife. He responded by becoming more irrational. Discussions always ended in an impasse. Sometimes, to keep the peace and avoid another standoff, I'd back off and agree with him. Since our joint account had become his personal slush fund, I started having the mortgage come out of my personal account, along with the phone bill and the electricity bill.

In year two of the marriage, he got suspended from work for drinking on the job. Well, drinking at lunch and then returning to the job. I didn't find out about it at first. He hid it well. Neighbors asked how Derrick was feeling one weekend, having seen him home that whole week. So, I asked Derrick more questions. I begged for him to confide in me. And when he wouldn't, I suggested we get help. He told me to mind my own business.

Maybe that is when I should have left, but I didn't.

Throughout our marriage there were countless times I referred to him as "Derrick MIA." He would go to a bar with friends and stay out all night. I would find hotel charges on the joint credit card. He would claim a friend used his card to book a room with a girl from the bar. I believed every word he said to me. He was a convincing liar. Other times he would go to guy's weekends at golf resorts, and when I called, I could hear women laughing in the background. I accepted his excuses that the women were with his friends and not with him.

There are 365 days in a year, and, on average, we had sex on 350 of them. Every year. For those years. Exceptions included sickness, being out of town, or his state of hangover. Even my period didn't keep him away. I rationalized there was no way he was having an affair if he was having that much sex at home.

In year four, he took up tennis and joined a tennis club. A fact I learned from the joint credit card statement. I reluctantly accepted his repeated absences on weekends and showed my approval by showering him with tennis gear and encouraging his new hobby.

Simultaneously, I bristled at the increase in his drinking. And the bitter mood that came with it. Derrick did not know how to be a happy drunk. The mere sight of me "killed his buzz," as he told me repeatedly, even in front of his friends. He would come home after a day at the club, with a friend driving his convertible for him, due to his inebriated state. They would walk in the door to whatever delights I had cooking on the BBQ and proceed to exclude me from their meal. Often, that suited me just fine.

Maybe that is when I should have left, but I didn't.

It took me another year to get up the courage to separate our bank accounts. I moved my pay deposit into my own account and had every bill moved to that same account. I couldn't trust Derrick to be responsible. I set up a schedule for him where he repaid me half of the household bills. The rest of his paycheck he could keep. It worked about 40% of the time.

That same year a charge for $3,000 from a legal firm appeared on one of our credit card statements. My tone changed. I peppered him with questions, demanded answers, and cut up his card. He admitted he was fighting an assault charge. He used those exact words: "fighting an assault charge." The irony of his choice of wording was lost on him.

With each inquiry Derrick became increasingly hostile. His tone and attitude were toxic toward me, but jovial toward his friends, people at group gatherings, and my family—toward whom he was especially kind.

Derrick, in the years I knew him as a partner, had never once washed the dishes after a meal in our home. He had never even offered. While in the presence of my parents, however, he was regularly ushering people out of the kitchen and scrubbing pots and pans, drying plates and cutlery, and wiping the appliances all without prompting. He was the guy who offered to help friends move, the guy who would rally a team on a Saturday to help patch a neighbor's roof, and the guy who always bought whatever someone's kid was selling. He never once raised a hand to me. But his words, they hurt.

In year six, he announced one Sunday while we were cozily watching a show we had recorded, "I wish I had never met you." He said it deadpan, without emotion and without making eye contact. I paused the show. He got up to grab another beer, and I left the room. From the other room, I heard the TV program resume and his beer bottle open.

Maybe that is when I should have left, but I didn't.

That same year his father died. Derrick flew home for the funeral and stayed for two months. I fully supported his need to tend to his widowed mother and the demands of the estate. His social media account told otherwise. Check-ins at bars in his hometown and pictures of women with their arms slung across his shoulder caused me embarrassment.

Throughout our marriage I confided in very few people. A friend or two might have heard various woes of being stood up for company Christmas parties or dinners at home. But it was never enough information to piece it all together, to help me see what I couldn't.

In year seven I saw a lawyer. Our beloved dog, that we'd adopted shortly after our elopement, had passed away suddenly. I quashed Derrick's suggestions to get a replacement pet. The process the lawyer laid out intimidated me. Divorce number one had been administratively simple, having been married only a short time. This one, however, sounded severe, and I wasn't sure I could weather it. I also didn't want to hurt Derrick.

Not long after that appointment with the lawyer, on a rare girl's weekend at a spa, a longtime friend in the group voiced that Derrick had once tried to force himself on her. It had happened early in my marriage and when she explained the circumstances, it all lined up. In spite of that, I asked her to repeat the story six times. Each time I heard it, more of the relationship puzzle pieces fell into place.

Maybe that is when I should have left, but I didn't.

When I returned home, I confronted him about the story. He denied it and questioned my friend's morality. Then he questioned mine. If I'd had any doubts about leaving him before, I didn't now. But I needed a plan. I now pictured a life after Derrick, and I *yearned* for it.

This time I saw a different lawyer. She was more welcoming, less intimidating, and seemed very "Team Rebekah." I explained that I wasn't looking to fleece Derrick, as I was the main breadwinner anyway and just wanted to take what was mine, sell the house, and leave. I even remained in the house, playing the doting wife, while my secret plan unfolded.

Derrick, however, suddenly started to spend more time at home. He became suspicious of my every move. He started going through my belongings, following my car, and texting my friends. He accused me of having an affair. He called my employer. Derrick was becoming unhinged. I told no one.

Halfway through our last year together, Derrick berated me in public. Once he even stood up in a restaurant near our home and drunkenly announced, "My wife is a slut" and "she is such a whore." During his rant, Derrick was escorted out of the restaurant.

Shell-shocked, I retreated to my car and left—both the restaurant and him.

***

It's funny how people feel the need to tell you things, things that would have been helpful, after you leave someone. After our separation, I was still in contact with mutual friends. In fact, I started seeing them like usual, except now I was alone. I brought salads to dinner parties, hosted birthday celebrations, and attended baby showers. But the stories about Derrick kept coming. In droves.

A friend of Derrick's, the husband of a couple we regularly saw, said to me, "So, you left because of his affairs?" Stunned, I nodded as the details were regurgitated to me. I nodded like it was old news. But it wasn't. It was new news. Painful news.

Another friend of Derrick's, whom I'd only met at the man's wedding, messaged me online and said he was proud of me leaving after finding out there were affairs the whole time we were together. Of course, he supplied a different example.

Derrick's sister used the phrase "boys will be boys" and inadvertently mentioned the long-term girlfriend Derrick had dated while he went home for their father's funeral. The same woman he had apparently been seeing throughout all the years of visiting his parents on the coast. Without me.

Then two of Derrick's coworkers came forward, eager to participate in the aftermath, asking me if our breakup was because of the two women he saw regularly when he claimed to be working overtime. One of whom he had even taken as his date to his company's Christmas party, the year I was home with the flu.

The last revelation, and probably the most devious and heartbreaking was that Derrick didn't actually play tennis. The club membership was a sham to give him an alibi to be away from me.

The news, and the evidence presented by all the examples, gutted me. It made me feel a fool, and I felt robbed of the past seven years. I was painfully aware of his efforts over the years to live a life separate from me. And with clear hindsight, I was able to piece together every one of his lies.

But that wasn't even why I left, because I learned all of that after the fact. I left because he wasn't *nice*. He wasn't *kind*. At least not to me.

In the end, he got the house, and I escaped hefty spousal payments. I started a new life in another town, rebuilding with the friends I had neglected during the time I was with Derrick and distancing myself from the ones I'd met though Derrick—the ones who'd known of Derrick's infidelity, had seen his erratic behavior, but had idly stood by without so much as a warning.

Almost one year after the ink had dried on our divorce, Derrick's body was found in the pool in his backyard. He had fallen asleep after one too many and had slipped beneath the surface. He was discovered by his fifth wife.

When I heard the news of his passing, I was conflicted. Not because the love was still there, or because I had even seen him since I left. But because he hadn't changed or learned from our disaster. But thankfully I had. (Or so I thought.)

20

NUMBER FORTY-FOUR

Guy number forty-four was my first online dating encounter. Our profiles matched and each of us swiped
right. Our first date at a well-lit restaurant dulled any
concerns of stranger-danger or nefarious abduction.
When Luke showed up, the first thing I noticed about
him was that he was tall—like basketball player tall. He
also had really nice hair and had worn a wrinkly but-
toned-down shirt that had been tucked casually into his
jeans. Even though the shirt was wrinkled, it worked
somehow.

Luke had that build that could pretty much make
anything look good. When he saw me at the entrance in
my leggings and long teal sweater that hit my curves in
all the right places, he smiled and gave me a hug. I was
grateful I'd worn my boots. Even with that extra height I
still only made it up to his chest.

With Luke there was none of that initial awkwardness
that you felt on most first dates. We pretty much just
clicked. The waitress checked how we were enjoying the

appetizer. He joked and told her it was our fifth wedding anniversary. I grinned back at him while I sipped my beer.

When she brought us a sparkler-topped cake after our meal, it was hard to keep a straight face. So when I giggled, Luke just squeezed my hand and said, "She's always like this when people make a fuss."

We lingered at the restaurant after the check was settled. I had insisted on paying half, but Luke wouldn't have it on account it was our "anniversary" and all. When we kissed at my car in the parking lot, I noticed he tasted like mint.

We texted when we got home and more dates followed. There was an evening at a comedy club where we found similarities in our humor while we poked fun at or commended the fearless amateur-night comedians. And there was that time we went to an IMAX theater where we both agreed the special effects were better than the plot. And another evening spent watching YouTube videos on TV, starting with the popular hits and gravitating to animals behaving as humans. We shared popcorn out of a bowl and cuddled in an oversized lounge chair.

Luke mentioned he had roommates, so we'd hang out in my home. I cooked foods that had stewed for hours in a crock pot, and we tried new recipes with each of us chopping vegetables and sipping chilled wine. On those cooking dates, I learned about his children. One was planned, one less so. Having never married, both children lived with their mother. He confided that most of his paycheck went to their care.

Our dates became adventures: laser tag, wine tastings, scenic Sunday drives, trips to the waterpark. With the exception of our first date, I always paid my share.

Luke's job had long hours, and it was challenging to find time in to see each other. Times when I was free, he was not. And the times he was free, I was at work. To add another variable to an already troubled equation, he saw his kids on alternate weekends.

Two months after "like at first sight," (his words, not mine), I hinted about seeing Luke's home.

"Maybe I should let you cook a meal for me, for a change!" I said one night.

"No, your place is better. Mine is a mess."

I pushed. I wanted to see where he lived. Our dates continued. I began to cover the expenses of our outings if I was the one planning them. While I thought it was a bit odd, I didn't mind covering his half. But when time had passed to the point where visiting his home could no longer be avoided, I began to insist on it. When he finally relented, he offered to cook dinner at his place.

His home was in a town known for its industry, rather than its residential neighborhoods. The house he lived in shined in perpetual daylight from the stadium-like flood lights that blazed from the gravel quarry down the street. As soon as I pulled up, I noticed the house was quite run-down. It was number 2641 on the street, but both the "2" and the "4" were gone. The remaining numbers lit up with empty spaces in between, like a grin missing a few teeth. Looking around I noticed the yard was overgrown and since the driveway was full of derelict cars, I was forced to park on the street.

The doorbell didn't work, but I remained positive and tried to overlook the shabby condition of the exterior of his home. He was a renter, after all. This was not his place. Unfortunately, when I stepped inside, I noticed it was equally in disrepair. Kitchen cupboards hung from one hinge or were missing entirely. When I looked down, there were noticeable stains on the carpet. I saw crumbs on the counter and unscraped dishes piled near the sink.

Determined to stay positive, I continued to forgive certain things, since he'd just cooked in that kitchen. But it turned out he hadn't. Dinner consisted of a roast chicken purchased precooked from the deli and a selection of sides in packaged containers. It was all good, but nothing was homemade. Perhaps he didn't have the cooking gene, which was forgivable. But it all left me curious about the mess.

Sitting on the couch, I was getting bites on my ankles. Fleas? I suggested we go out for dessert. Maybe ice cream? He said there was nothing nearby. More scratching. I was definitely getting bitten by something. Bed bugs?

On my way to the washroom, I peeked into his bedroom. I saw a twin bed, a desk, and a large chest of drawers and some laundry in a basket near the dresser. As

I scanned the room I noticed there was no closet. And where did his kids sleep when they visited?

Even having seen most of the house, I was not prepared for what awaited me when I walked into his bathroom. I was horrified. I'd seen better facilities in airports in foreign lands. After a giant roach crawled into the sink, I decided my bladder could wait.

I returned downstairs, slowly, not sure what to say. Back in the living room I was speechless, still processing the evening's disappointing reveal. And words escaped me when he asked if I wanted to stay over. I simply stood up and told him I was thankful for dinner and that I was going to get on my way. I offered to do something the following week and gave him a hasty peck on the cheek, in lieu of our usual goodbye entanglement.

All the way home, I had a one-person debate in my head. He rents. It's not his home. He can't control the appearance. Except that he could. He may not be able to decide on cabinets or types of hedges. But he can rake, he can fix, he can clean. It was the lack of pride, not the income inequity that baffled me. Was he proud to show that home to his children?

By the time I'd reached home, Luke had left a message on my voicemail, essentially ending our life as a couple. I guess my poker face had failed me. He wasn't angry or accusing in the voicemail. He sounded sullen. He told me it had happened before and that he understood.

I called him back and got his voicemail. I told him it wasn't over. I said we needed to talk. A great deal of soul-searching followed. I even sought counsel in friends. I remained optimistic and told others while simultaneously trying to convince myself: "This can totally work." "He's so nice." "We get along so well."

But it was clear this couldn't work—not long-term—at least not on the level that I'd hoped. Sure, we could continue to date, spending time at my place. I could keep paying for him. But this would never permit a solid partnership or a relative equality. And I couldn't continue with someone who could allow himself or his children to live in an environment that lacked care.

Many things in his situation were beyond his control, but many were not. It was the latter that I was most disappointed in.

Luke never called me back, and as I cruised through my home from one clean room to the next, I understood why.

21

NUMBER FIFTY-FOUR

Guy number fifty-four caused me to send a flurry of texts to my girlfriends. It was too juicy to hold back. I had been treating myself to regular therapeutic massages. Ninety minutes of luxury that I received once a month at a clinic near my home. I booked my appointment online, chose my timeslot, treatment, and therapist—all with the click of a button. The hours of the clinic were great, and the monthly indulgence suited my lifestyle.

Some customers disliked the scheduling system, because there was no guarantee you would get the same therapist each time you went. Whereas, I didn't care. My only preference was a male therapist. Not for erotic reasons. It's just, in my experience, I found female therapists applied too much pressure and I left feeling battered, not relaxed. Over the years, I had found that men responded better to my requests for "light pressure" and didn't try to knead me into oblivion.

At the clinic, the rates were super cheap, yet the therapists were all experienced and licensed. The catch was you had to commit to twelve massages a year and pay monthly, whether you got a massage or not. And when the schedule booked up quickly online, sometimes it was hard to find a timeslot.

It was around month number nine of this yearlong commitment when I had a massage by a therapist named Regis. He was young, fit, and very keen. I had previously seen his name on the schedule, but it was my first time as his client. He asked me the usual questions at the start of the session about my goals for the session, my health status, and what I did for a living. After giving him a list of problem areas, I added that my calves had been stinging since a recent long-distance run and asked him to spend some extra time there.

After intake, he left me to disrobe, and I made myself comfortable facedown on the massage table under the sheets. I was pretty laissez-faire about disrobing and often chucked my clothes into a pile on the chair and then hopped on the table, ready for my treatment about twenty seconds after the therapist had left the room. I heard the usual light knock on the door asking if I was ready. I mumbled yes and he entered the room, performing the customary prep of dimming the lights, adjusting the sheets, and washing his hands.

He apologized for his cold hands, and I heard him pump the massage oil onto his palms from his waistband holster. He started with my back. My neck and shoulders followed. I was already drifting in and out of consciousness. I am not a talker during a massage, something I let the therapists know. The way I see it I am there to relax, not make new friends.

I breathed deeply as he continued his work. He moved the top sheet to access my legs. I should add—with a respectful nod to all the licensed massage therapists out there who have figured out how to wrangle the sheets to allow the client as much privacy as possible—that is no small feat. I, however, had no concern in this area and often found in my massages, by a variety of practitioners, that the sheet game was not always played consistently. I had therapists who used my spine and butt cheek separation as the division leaving the left side of my body entirely exposed while my right was covered and vice versa. I had a therapist once take the entire sheet off me, shake it in the air, and then cover me in a different area. None of this had bothered me. I just found it curious that the practice of draping could be so different.

On this occasion, his massage of my legs was just what I needed. It was relieving the tight muscles from my running-without-ever-stretching routine and was very relaxing. While he was massaging my thighs, I thought I felt his hand graze one inner thigh a little high up. And as he continued, I noted a few more grazes.

Soon after I was on my back. This is the part of the massage when the therapist holds the sheet more as a shield from seeing anything than to cover the client. I flipped over, and the sheet was replaced on my body, now faceup.

The massage continued with some great work on my arms, legs, and my favorite part: the foot. No lie, I could probably schedule a ninety-minute foot massage and be just as satisfied in the end. When he was done with my feet, Regis offered a scalp massage, which I declined. Not because I was concerned with messy hair, but rather I wasn't a fan of someone massaging my feet and then touching my hair.

At the end of the session, he cautioned me to get up slowly and said he would be waiting with a glass of water outside. I dressed and joined him near the reception desk. After exchanging pleasantries I was on my way.

I texted my friend from the car, saying *I think I was just grazed in a massage.* I gave her the details and recounted the experience. *I think you just haven't had sex in a while and are imagining sex where it isn't,* was my friend's witty comeback.

To be honest, I didn't give it much thought. The next month, the online massage schedule was pretty booked, and I was forced to take an appointment with a girl whose name I did not recognize. This girl was all business and despite my repeated requests for her to lighten the pressure, it never happened. At the halfway point, during the flipover, I told her I was done. She didn't understand. When I told her I wasn't feeling well and didn't need to continue, she ended the session. I left unsatisfied and a little disgruntled. She hadn't even offered me a glass of water on my way out.

The following month, month eleven of my twelve-month commitment, I almost skipped my appointment. I had left it until late in the month to book my slot and by the time I got online I figured I wouldn't have any luck finding a spot. To my surprise, there was an opening that evening. With Regis.

Regis recognized me in the waiting area and called me back to the room. Since he'd seen me before, we were able to skip the whole health questionnaire portion of the appointment. Also, because he had worked on me before, he asked different questions like if I liked the music or if he should turn it down and whether the lighting was OK. He also offered me a heating pad under my back, which I gladly accepted.

Then the massage got underway. It was once again very relaxing. I always marveled at how easily I could fall asleep during massages. Although, again, while face down and having my legs massaged, I swear Regis grazed my inner thigh. Was I still imagining this?

I didn't move. Not out of fear. Trust me, I can handle myself and if I'd had any issue with what was being done to my body, I would have been up off that table, and Regis would be reeling in the corner. But I didn't have any problem with his technique. Besides, I wasn't even sure what it was yet.

As the massage continued, my inner thighs were unquestionably getting attention. And then, there it was.

A definite semi penetration into the vagina. Yep, it happened. And I remember, clear to this day, saying to myself, "This is happening!" I wasn't opposed. Jesus, I was thrilled. This is what they talked about in movies and books about shady massage places, usually referencing male clients, where "happy endings" were offered.

And here I was, experiencing it! Without prompting, his fingers were inside me, and I let out a muffled moan of pleasure. He caressed my lower back and whispered in my ear, "You OK?"

I giggled, "A little late to ask permission."

This continued for a few minutes and was an over-the-top hot experience. Then he smiled and asked if I was able to stay quiet, and I nodded. God, I would have removed my vocal cords at that point if it meant it could continue.

At some point I turned over to be faceup, the sheets went missing, and he was undressed, too. Hello! When did his clothes come off? I had already climaxed from his fingers just being inside me and then he asked if I wanted to have sex. I was just about to ask about a condom when he showed me one in his hand. This was not his first rodeo. I said something resembling, "hell, yes." And it happened. Right there on the massage table, and up against the wall, and partially on a chair.

I was dizzy afterward from the sex frenzy. When I got dressed and opened the door, never was I so glad to see a glass of water. On the way out, he thanked me and said,

"Have a great weekend," like someone would say to any client.

I smiled and said, "You, too" and paid my check and left.

Now, this story was too good to keep to myself. I texted the same friend, and a few others, and explained what had just happened. Of the five I texted, four were both envious and excited. Only one was appalled—a pretty good balance, I think.

I have to admit, on that day and on the days that followed where I reimagined the scene, it was the most sensual experience I had ever encountered. Hands down. It topped any sexy one-night fling, any encounter with a longtime lover, and any book I had ever read.

My friends joked, "Does that mean you just paid for sex?" to which I said, "No, I claimed it under my company's health benefits, so technically I just *expensed* sex."

I changed massage therapy clinics after that. Not because I was embarrassed or ashamed. But because I wanted to keep the memory alive and didn't want to tarnish it. And because, after all, I really wanted a massage.

Most of the time.

22

FRY GUY

A New Year's trip to Cancun left me tanned, well-rested, and with a great New Year's Eve story. The all-inclusive resort came by way of recommendation of a friend, who'd stayed there about half a dozen times over the years as an end-of-school celebration with her daughter each June. I was familiar with the chain of resorts and the online reviews were positive. After booking my trip I was stoked! This trip was just what I needed, and by the time New Year's came around my suitcase was fully packed and ready to go.

I arrived early on December 28th and as soon as I got to my room, I started unpacking my luggage, which consisted primarily of bikinis, short dresses, high heels, and sunscreen. Once dressed in proper beach attire, I toured the property and found a spot in the Platinum class section of the beach.

The description of the luxuries of Platinum status far outweighed the reality. Sure, our section had the newer beach loungers and an exclusive bar and did not permit kids. However, its location was a mere twenty-five feet from the other bar, the other beach, and all the kids. So, it turned out to be not as secluded as the pictures had led me to believe. And the beach service was nonexistent, leaving many of us to joke that perhaps *we* were the beach service, resulting in one of us regularly calling to the others in the area, "I'm going to the bar, who needs something?"

Over the first few days, my routine consisted of an early trip to the shore, to catch the sunrise. An older man, part of a couple who had been to the resort over forty times, had started putting a single lounge chair in my preferred location after day two. We exchanged our "good mornings," as he set out to arrange the remaining loungers into the preferred configuration of those he had met. I joked that he should be paid for his work. He just smiled and studied the loungers, making sure they were precisely the way he wanted them.

The food had yet to impress me and the slow service was consistent with what I was accustomed to in the laid-back Caribbean. Despite this, I was having a great time and was already reading my second novel of the trip. Each day the entertainment staff came around asking people to sign up and pay for the New Year's Eve gala. I listened to the compelling account of previous years' events by the couple who had attended many in their forty-plus-year history with the resort. After hearing that the evening consisted of a performance by a local children's choir during the meal and a single glass of champagne at midnight, I realized the gala was not for me. There was no dancing afterward, and, according to the seasoned couple, people dispersed immediately after the clock struck twelve. Not exactly my idea of a good time. Midnight is typically when things start getting interesting.

So, I went to the tour-booking office at the resort seeking an alternate plan. At first, I got the hard sell about the resort party, which I had expected. The resort clearly made a profit on the $100 per couple price tag, a price that would not be reduced even though I was half a couple. They were also extremely proud of their event and couldn't understand why I did not want to attend.

That's when a member of the entertainment staff wandered into the air-conditioned tour office, likely in search of a reprieve from the heat, and overheard our discussion. He suggested a few bars in Cancun that were having New Year's events but warned me that tickets were selling fast.

I Googled each option while standing in the office, selecting the one that best fit my needs. After giving them the info, they called the bar and bought a ticket in my name. The staff warned me it was an expensive thirty-minute cab ride away. I was further warned to go very early, because the bar routinely oversold their tickets and even holding one did not guarantee entry. I paused briefly, weighing the pros and cons of arriving at the bar only to be turned away. Was it worth the risk? Well, it definitely beat the sedate event planned by the resort, so I decided to take my chances.

Two days later I was in a cab heading to the bar at 7:00 p.m. I decided to ask the driver about getting a cab ride back: "Will it be busy just after midnight?"

He indicated that it would not be busy then, because "the party was not over" until about 4:00 a.m. He said by 4:00, I might have to wait a while for a ride.

"Thanks," I said, knowing it would be unlikely that I'd stay out that late.

When I got to the bar and displayed my ticket, I was granted entry with a neon handstamp of a palm tree. I found a place at the bar, next to two women who were eating dinner and chatting. There were a few full tables of families having dinner, but for the most part, the place was empty.

I ordered a glass of champagne. Then I asked for a menu and tipped the bartender $20 on my first drink. I wanted to be well looked-after even after the crowds hit. My tip, and the smaller tips that followed, worked. My glass was refilled often, and my check at the end of the night reflected only about half of what I consumed.

Not long after my first glass of champagne, the place started getting crowded. I remember looking up from my menu and suddenly not being able to see the front door through the sea of people. Most tables were occupied by that point, and those who were not staying for the party started to pay their checks and exit. A group of men took the remaining seven seats at the bar to my left. Each ordered something to eat and drink. They conversed animatedly in Spanish.

As the bar was filling up, I struck up a conversation with the two ladies to my right. They were visiting from Central America, and we were excited about their experiences in Mexico. They included me in their group as we took selfies and talked about the evening ahead. Part of our game was people-watching, and the group of guys seated at the bar were on these ladies' radar.

The guy to my immediate left was eating something that looked delicious and the temptation to grab one of his fries was strong. Not knowing his reaction and being in a foreign country, I resisted. My desire to order my own food had come and gone. I actually was content existing on the lunch I'd eaten earlier at the resort. When I mentioned I was jonesing for one of his fries, the women joked that I should ask him for one. But I held out.

The fries were not to be.

Around the time that my neighbor's plate was cleared away by the bartender, one of the other men from his group approached me and struck up a conversation. I learned they were all friends, from another part of Mexico, vacationing at the beach for the holidays. There were seven of them. I asked him about their jobs. As I studied them, I figured they were about fifteen years younger than me.

Around 10:00 p.m. the DJ and the strobe lights were in full effect. There was a dance floor, complete with an elevated dance stage, at the end of the room, not far from my seat at the bar. A few people were starting to occupy the stage, and the main dance area was crowded. A door was propped open on the opposite side, which led to the beach and the ferry docks where you could watch passengers line up to catch a ferry to Cozumel. The beach was very well lit in front of the bar and the party overflowed outside. I checked it out briefly, while the ladies at the bar saved my place.

When I returned to my seat, I saw they were still there, although they were now standing with their purses in their hands. When I asked if they were leaving, one of them said, "My sister isn't feeling well—too much to drink."

"Oh no, that's too bad," I said. "Nice meeting you both."

We hugged. They asked whether I was OK to stay at the bar by myself, and I quickly reassured them they were not dampening my plans. I had come alone, after all. The unwell sister apologized, and then they left.

I resumed my spot at the bar and debated giving up my seat to go mingle. The seven men had surrendered their seats to a few couples and were now in a small cluster near the hallway to the restrooms. One couple mistook the area for their own personal space and had their belongings strewn across a good portion of the bar.

Another glass of champagne appeared in front of me, freshly poured by the bartender. Soon after, a member of the group of men approached me and asked why I didn't leave with my friends. I explained I had only met the ladies that night and didn't really know them. After the usual round of questions about me traveling alone, he introduced me to the group. I heard their names but knew the information would not stay with me long. The loud venue and their accents made that impossible.

The group of seven ebbed and flowed as each of the men either used the restroom, went outside for a smoke, or went to dance. I danced a few times with one guy who was dressed very chic with a fashionable button-down shirt where the design on the cuffs and collar differed from the main pattern. He looked classy. He was also a stupendous dancer. My quality of rhythm did not match his, but I had a great time trying.

During one of our dance breaks, a different member of the group suggested I drink a glass of water. I'm not sure if he was referring to my sweatiness from dancing or from seeing my constant champagne refills. I agreed, and we muscled up to the bar for a glass of ice water each. The bartender served us with breakneck speed, to the chagrin of those waiting three-people-deep for service. I explained the reason to my water partner.

I rejoined their group, which I was now referring to in my head as the seven dwarfs. My label was not derogatory in nature, and it had nothing to do with their stature. It was because each of them was playing a different role, and I felt like Snow White. There was the one I danced with, the one who brought me water a few more times that evening, the one who made sure I got a crown and feather boa when the party favors were handed out, the one who didn't say much and kept to himself, the one who got me a drink refill each time we went to the bar, and the one whose fry I had almost stolen.

Around 11:30 p.m., great-dancer guy planted a kiss on me while I stood near the bar looking at the crowd. I laughed but said to him, quite directly, "You can't do that. You can't just kiss a girl without making sure she's into you. You can get into trouble."

By his expression, I sensed he hadn't meant any harm. He had just overstepped.

Then he asked, "Will you kiss me at midnight?"

I remember saying, "No, you just had your kiss."

If he was disappointed, he handled it well. We danced again and he asked, "Do you want to kiss anyone here?"

I was surprised by his directness, but also found it charming. Understanding I wouldn't know anyone here in a few hours from now, I said, "Yes, one of your friends."

He asked which one, and I disclosed my interest in "fry guy," the one who had sat next to me while he ate. What seemed like only seconds later, fry guy was at my side having been waved over by "great dancer." They spoke briefly in Spanish. I ignored the obvious awkwardness of the moment. Great dancer disappeared, and I was left standing there with fry guy.

I asked if he wanted to dance to which he said, "nah" and suggested we walk outside on the beach instead.

That was when I said "nah."

Not that the beach wasn't gorgeous or that there wasn't a lure to go out there, but I was keenly aware of my experiences in the Dominican Republic and wanted to stay where I was familiar. And the bartender was keeping tabs on me. She frequently asked me if I was doing OK and whether anyone was bothering me. I felt in control in the bar. The beach was an unknown factor I didn't need.

Fry guy and I chatted by the bar, and he managed to secure a seat despite the crowd. He sat and I semi-danced and swayed to the music while standing between his parted legs. Close to midnight I turned and faced him, and we kissed. We did the countdown to New Year's, him in Spanish and me in English. We threw confetti and clinked glasses with the other "dwarfs." I think we probably only said about twenty words to each other, but it was charged, and it was the perfect New Year's moment.

And just like we did in our pre-midnight play, everyone's roles resumed. Water was brought to me by "water dwarf," my champagne was ordered by "drink dwarf," I danced with "great dancer," and I kissed "fry guy."

And at 3:30 a.m., the seventh dwarf, another one I had only really waved to, helped me get my check and waited with me for my cab to arrive. I had asked the bartender to tell the driver where I was going to avoid any confusion. The other six men hovered nearby. And as the cab door closed, all seven waved to me and fry guy and great dancer each blew me a kiss.

No numbers were assigned on my list because my intimacy with fry guy was only a kiss, but they all get an honorable mention for treating me like royalty.

23

NUMBER THIRTY-SEVEN

Guy number thirty-seven got me fired from my job.

This job was in a different city, and I had recently moved close to the office, having done some minor renovations to my new home before my first day of work. It was a small two-level house on a well-worn street that was a little too close to a major roadway. The sounds of the cars and buses took some time getting used to when I lay in bed each night.

I focused on upgrading the interior when I first moved in. The garden and porch would have to come later. It was sold to me as a one bedroom plus den, but I realized after moving in that the master suite must have originally been two separate rooms, given the different flooring in that one space. Perhaps I could renovate the flooring later, but for now it was "livable," just in time for me to start my new job.

The new city introduced the cumbersome task of finding a new dentist, hairdresser, favorite grocery store, and local eatery. All the familiar ones were too far away for regular use. It was at a local mom-and-pop restaurant where I met number thirty-seven.

We were both waiting at the hostess stand to collect our takeout. My order came out first and the hostess called out my name and "two fish tacos and a side of calamari." While he was waiting for his order, the man pointed to my paper takeout bag saying, "Oh, the fish tacos...they are really good here." I smiled and headed to the door, deliberately slowing so I could hear his name called by the hostess. "Rowan? Mussels and fish tacos?" I held the door for him as I exited, and he called as he approached his car, "Enjoy your dinner, Rebekah."

My new job was a project-based position for a shipping a logistics company, and although they paid me directly, I was not an employee "on the books" and did not have an office or any staff that reported to me. I was, however, issued a company cell phone and laptop, for which I was thankful. My previous cell phone was returned to my last company when I left and my personal laptop was in pretty sad shape, after a recent spill that happened while I was charging it on the kitchen counter.

The work was fairly rewarding. I oversaw the proposed restructuring for five of their locations and was tasked with creating a plan to boost efficiencies for the coming year. The locations were all within two hours of my new home. I visited them on different days and sequestered myself in a conference room if I didn't have any meetings. I mostly saw warehouse buildings, shippers, and a few maintenance personnel. It was in one of those visits to a warehouse that I officially met Rowan, the Warehouse Manager and eater of mussels and fish tacos.

24

A few months later we were all invited to the company fundraiser, which was an annual outdoor event. Even though it was held on a Saturday, I noticed that most of the staff had made an appearance. Many brought their families, including small children. The children had their faces painted, threw water balloons, and participated in field games. Not having a family was always noticeable at these events. I was intensely aware that I was not cheering any young one on at the egg race or balloon toss. But I also saw it as a chance to get credit for making an appearance before slipping away early.

I walked up next to Rowan and nearly got a spatula in the ribs as he worked the grill.

"Sorry, Rebekah. I didn't see you there. I'm feeding the masses."

"I see that. Can I help with anything?"

Rowan smiled and gave me the task of placing cooked burgers and hot dogs in the appropriate buns and passing them to the next person who then added salad and passed them along the line.

I was busy with my bun duties for the next hour or so. I hadn't even realized what time it was until I felt a tap on my shoulder and turned to see Rowan holding a plate with a fully dressed burger and a hot dog along with some salad and plastic cutlery.

"Let's get ourselves something to eat. These guys have it under control."

"Do you want the burger or the hot dog? Or are you one of those salad-only girls who steal food off guys' plates?"

I laughed. "Maybe we can split them?"

Rowan proceeded to cut the burger and hot dog in equal halves using one of the plastic knives. Our first bites settled in. We were quiet, but not in an awkward way. And the noise of the field games, complete with cheers and frequent shouts from children, filled in the gaps. Then he asked about the job and my boss, Edith.

"Has Edith got you doing any of her dirty work?" he inquired.

"Dirty work?" I asked.

"You know, recommending her enemies be fired, promoting her friends. She's got a real hate on for her boss."

"Nothing that interesting, I'm sorry to report."

When Rowan realized he wasn't going to get anything juicy on Edith, he asked how I was doing after my move to the city. When we'd first met at work, about four months ago, we had talked briefly about my move. But in this informal setting I felt I could go into more detail about all the renovations I'd done when I first moved in. He asked a lot of questions about the flooring products, including how they were installed. He seemed to really know the process. I told him my additional reno plans and how I was thinking about possibly adding a bedroom and redoing the porch.

As I was sharing my plans, Rowan nodded: "I'm constantly swinging a hammer at my place. It never stops. If you ever need a hand with anything, just say the word."

I thanked him for the offer: "I could never do that to you. Before you know it, you would be a general contractor on my staff and spend more time at my house than your own."

Rowan grinned: "Well, that wouldn't be so bad."

I didn't know how to respond. I mean Rowan was definitely very handsome, but I wasn't sure about his situation. I presumed he was unattached as I saw no ring. And he didn't bring anyone to the BBQ. After weighing all the different options in my head, I decided to just let the comment pass.

We sat and watched the crowds for a few minutes longer and then sought out a garbage bin for the plate and forks. I thanked him for the company at lunch and then walked toward the field where the games were taking place. I saw some staff members participating with their families and another staff member from the Marketing department taking photos of all the action. I smiled, thinking that kids in potato sacks would end up on some future brochure for the company.

Later that evening, when I got back from my run, I saw a new text message on my cell phone. It was from a number I didn't recognize.

It said: *Thanks for lunch today*. With an emoji of a hamburger. And a plastic knife.

Rowan!

I responded back. *Thank YOU. You made lunch.*

About a week later, while I was holed up in the board-room working on a change to the shipping scheduling system, I saw another text come in on my phone.

I see your car is at the main office today. Free for lunch?

There had been no text exchanges with Rowan since the initial one with the emoji.

I quickly texted him back: *Can't today; duty calls.*

He countered with: *After work? Quick drink before you head home?*

I didn't respond at first. I needed to give it some thought. Did I want to start something up with a some-one from work? He was awful cute, but...

An hour later, I texted Rowan: *OK*.

Later that afternoon Rowan came to the main office and popped his head in the boardroom. "Where you wanna go?" And then he flashed that winning smile. The same one I had gotten right after he almost impaled me at the BBQ. I grinned, surprising myself that he had this impact on me.

"How about Harley's Barn at five?"

He nodded and then I turned my attention back to the spreadsheets I was working on. I have to admit it was hard to focus. I kept checking my phone to see if it was time to head out.

Harley's parking lot was completely full when I arrived, so I had to park at the church next door, where the lot was completely vacant. Rowan was standing near the bar talking to two men when I arrived. It was a heated, but amiable, discussion about a sports team. I noticed that Rowan had changed his clothes, and his weathered warehouse uniform was replaced with crisp dark jeans and a beige t-shirt with a logo of a local brewery. His sandy blond hair looked wet, as if he'd just showered, and was combed neatly off his face.

He looked over at me as I walked up and smiled. He immediately dropped out of his sports discussion and removed himself from the group. The men looked my way and raised their beer bottles as a hello. I didn't recognize them as employees at the company and smiled politely in response.

Rowan and I grabbed two beers at the bar and then squeezed into an area not far from where he and his friends had been a few minutes earlier. We sipped our beers straight from the bottle. He mentioned his son was playing football that night, and he had some time before he had to leave to pick him up. I asked him about his kids, their ages, all the while trying to figure out Rowan's approximate age.

I noticed there was no mention of a wife. And he used "I" a lot, saying things like, "I have some time before I pick up Ryan. I spend most of the weekend shuttling Jessica around. I didn't get much sleep last night, because I

155

was fixing Jessica's bike tire first thing this morning, so she could ride to school."

I couldn't help but notice "we" was not used in reference to his home life. While we were chatting, Rowan was jostled by someone walking to the bar who also bumped into me as we were finishing our beers. I noticed that he didn't move all the way back to his original position afterward. As we raised our bottles for our last sips, our hands were touching each other. I didn't move either. It was nice to have this moment of quiet intimacy in the middle of a noisy bar.

When it was time to go, there was a slight pause as we set our empty bottles on the bar and looked at each other. I got the sense that he, like me, didn't really want to go yet, but we weren't going to have another drink, because we were both driving. Thankfully, Rowan broke the awkwardness by asking, "Where did you park? When I got here, I had to park practically at the church." I told him I was parked by the church, too, and he joked about killing two birds with one stone and going to a service after going to a bar.

We went our separate directions, partway across Harley's parking lot and he said, "See you soon, I hope, Rebekah."

I nodded, "Thanks for the beer. Have a great night."

It was all very PG, and I stewed about it that evening, trying to dissect his actions to glean any

deeper meaning. Finally, I had to accept there just wasn't any deeper meaning. There may be something, but there might not. But I hoped there was.

One night, while passing through my living room with a basket of laundry, my cell phone rang. *Rowan* appeared on the screen from its spot on the ottoman. I presumed it was an accidental dialing, as he'd never phoned me before after work, so I didn't answer.

I heard the distinctive beep of a new voicemail from the laundry room. I didn't even turn on the dryer before I ran to grab the phone to listen to the message.

"What are you doing for dinner tomorrow night? I bet you're likely eating something while standing over the sink," he said, like he was having a conversation with himself. "I think I might have a better deal for you than that. Let me take you to dinner."

25

We met up for dinner at a casual chain restaurant about halfway between our two homes. Rowan and I shared an appetizer and washed it down with some wine. I was surprised at how easily our conversation flowed. After dinner, we lingered over dessert. We had each ordered a different dessert and put them in the center of the table to share. I said he should have saved the plastic knife from the charity event, so he could carve the desserts in half for us. Then Rowan leaned closer: "My God, I wanted to kiss you so badly that day."

Upon hearing that my heart fluttered, and our relationship progressed quickly.

We saw, or talked to, each other daily after that. Our phones blew up constantly with calls and texts. We created short forms of communication with each other, half texts that conveyed our whole thoughts. We each had nicknames. He'd bring coffee to me without prompting on a busy morning, between meetings. He fixed a few things at my house, often without me even asking. We celebrated ridiculous anniversaries like "our 12th business meeting together" and our 50th date.

While our verbal communications were 100% professional in meetings and in-person at work, they were less professional, and downright steamy, by text.

We didn't see each other socially on weekdays, usually due to his shift, or his kids' schedules. We did get together every other weekend, when he didn't have to "parent," as he phrased it. Sometimes he stayed over. More often, though, he went home at the end of our dates.

He and his wife, from whom he was separated, had an unusual agreement. They each had the kids half the time and instead of shuttling the kids back and forth to a different home every few days, the opposite parent would move in and out of the house. When it was not their turn with the kids, there was an apartment they shared and would use when not staying at the family home. Rowan said their paths never crossed, and they communicated by text, notes, and the rare phone call. I had overheard a couple of those calls. They were very matter of fact and cold.

His unusual living situation didn't matter to me. I wasn't begging to move in together, and I had no intention of meeting his kids until we were much further into the relationship. It was important to me that our connection, and whatever it was going to grow to be, was cemented first. Rowan wasn't in a hurry to introduce his kids to me either, for similar reasons. He suggested that since his separation was only a year ago, the kids may not be very welcoming to a new person in their life just yet. I appreciated that Rowan didn't want to set me up to fail.

Since I was genuinely interested about his life, I routinely asked questions about his children, and he shared lots of pictures of them at different activities. He made and took calls with them during our time together. I asked questions about his living arrangement, expressing empathy that he really had no space to call his own and that it must be unnerving to share the same bed (albeit on different days) with an ex. He would mostly shrug and say something like, "It is what it is" whenever I pressed him on this topic. So, I dropped my questions after a while.

We both agreed to keep our relationship quiet at work. It was for two reasons really. First, I had some influence over the recommendations for the structure of the organization, and we didn't want anyone to perceive a conflict of interest. And then there was Edith's boss who'd recently started mentioning a VP position that I might be suited for. I was genuinely interested in the job, and I didn't want to make him think that my loyalties were divided. If he did offer me the job, and Rowan and I were still together, I decided I would make it known then.

Due to our relationship being under wraps, at work events we were friendly but not overly so. We were still practically inseparable, texted a million times during the day, met for lunch when our schedules permitted, but we never touched, kissed, or spoke unprofessionally in the workplace. And we were good at our charade.

Or so we thought.

Truth be told, all the sexy texting had taken up a bit of my time over the past three months, and I hadn't been as diligently focused as I had once been. I vowed to step it up and present significant progress at our next meeting. I was openly suspicious of Edith now both from stories Rowan told me as well as my own observations, so I didn't mention to Edith about the VP idea that had been floated by me.

Time passed. My contract was extended for another year. The extension came just two months before the original contract was to expire. I was told the extension was to ensure my entire project was complete before I moved into the VP role, which was now considered a done deal.

Rowan and I had been in each other's lives for a while, and our fascination with each other hadn't waned. If anything, I was the one putting on the brakes at work, trying to text less, so I could prove myself.

Rowan knew of the VP role that was in my future. He would often joke, "When you are president, I will become your Executive Assistant, and we can rule the empire."

Our texts often continued the same line of humor, saying things like: *Hey VP-in-waiting, let's grab lunch.* Or: *If only Edith knew you were the one she should be watching.* Most of the teasing came from him, but I willingly participated.

Weeks later, Edith sent me an email asking me to present my analysis that afternoon. Her boss was in town. And she asked that I meet them in her office and bring all the project material. I found it strange, since I didn't have any significant new progress to update since our last meeting.

I texted Rowan to share my concerns. He responded with: *Don't worry about it. She probably just wants you to investigate her next target.*

I tried to laugh, appreciating his levity.

But when I arrived at the meeting, something felt off. I sat down and opened my laptop to the latest project update summary. The other open tabs on my computer contained the various levels of supporting analysis and proposed directions we could take. Edith was at her desk. And I noticed her boss was standing, which struck me as odd. Then I noticed Edith had several sheets of paper displayed across her desk, all laid out next to each other, so much so, that hardly any of the top of her desk was visible.

As I leaned to put my bag on the chair next to me, something on the paper nearest to me caught my eye.

Are you wearing panties under that skirt?

I can't believe we sat that close in the meeting and didn't end up touching.

I can smell your perfume on my sweater.

There were printed texts between me and Rowan. Dozens of them. All on Edith's desk. *Oh God.* I could feel my face burn. My mouth turned dry. I set the laptop down on top of some of the pages, knowing that we wouldn't be going over the project plan. Edith picked up one of the pages near her and read it aloud: *Edith would die if she knew we used the project plan as a placemat.* That was a night where Rowan stopped by with dinner, and I had the pages spread out on the ottoman.

I cleared my throat. I didn't look at anyone. The wait was worse than whatever was coming.

And that's when Edith unleashed on me, "Can't meet deadlines. Spends company time on personal affairs. Texting during work hours. Conflict of interest. Unprofessional behavior in the office. Sabotage." She said each statement deliberately, almost spitting the emphasis of the words right at me.

Wait! (I wanted to say.)

What you're saying isn't true! (I should have said.)

Sabotage? (I wanted to question.)

"Having an affair with a married man," she spat.

He's separated. (I should have corrected.)

I finally found my voice.

"I am sorry to have disappointed you both, but my relationship with Rowan has no bearing on my work here. I have worked very hard and have proven myself to you both. I am a worthy asset to this company. Edith, you said last month that you were so grateful for me being here."

And then my mind came to a screeching halt. *Wait. Why had she been through our texts?*

Everything was happening so fast, it seemed like the room was spinning. Before I could say anything else, Edith scooped up all the pages from the table into a messy pile and took the laptop from me and closed the lid. She asked for my company-issued phone, my only active phone, and I handed it over. No doubt she would see more texts from Rowan since I'd arrived at the meeting. Man, I had to warn him. No sense in both of us getting fired over this. But I had no way to reach him.

I nodded, put my bag on my shoulder and turned to leave. I was fighting back tears. Edith stood and opened the door for me. Her boss stared at the ground. Still silent. Was he inferior around Edith, too?

Edith and I walked quietly to the main entrance of the building. As the sliding doors opened for me, she muttered in almost a hushed tone, "And wake up, dear. He's not separated."

26

I went home. Devastated.

I had just lost my current job, my VP promotion, and learned Rowan was not separated. I'm not sure which piece of information upset me the most. While at home, I wondered if Rowan knew about me already. I wondered if he had unknowingly sent me more incriminating texts that Edith might have seen. I wondered if he also got fired. And I wondered if he had been lying to me. As much as I wanted to confront him, I also wanted him to comfort me. But without a phone or a laptop, I wasn't going to reach him that night.

I woke up around 4:00 a.m. At first, I didn't recall what had happened. Then it came rushing back. And the tears flowed. So many tears. Crying so much that I struggled to catch my breath. I splashed cold water on my face. Then traded that for a hot shower. I stood under the hot flow of water for half an hour.

I lay on the couch and saw a t-shirt of Rowan's folded on top of the laundry basket nearby. I tried to clear my mind by streaming some shows on Netflix. Nothing resonated. I tried a hot drink. A cold drink. A cold beer. And then I cried some more.

I must have fallen asleep. When I woke up, it was noon. I was worried that poor Rowan was going crazy, wondering what had happened to me. I needed a phone. I wasn't ready to ask to borrow one from a neighbor, because I'd have to explain what happened to mine.

So, I went to the mall that afternoon and bought a new phone and monthly plan. I didn't even pay attention to the options. I just got one that closely resembled the device I had just handed over the previous day.

I hadn't even left the store when I texted Rowan's work phone, the only number I had for him. *Rowan, it's me. They have my phone. Don't text using your work phone. Call me at this number.*

I waited on a bench in the mall, near the mobile phone outlet. Thirty minutes. No response.

I called his phone. It went to voicemail.

Oh God, did he get fired? Are they reading his texts now?

I waited and tried calling again. It went straight to voicemail. I didn't dare leave a message.

I went back home, and this time I tried comfort in the form of a hot bubble bath and soothing music. More tears came.

When had I last eaten?

The light on my new phone flashed while I was making an omelet. It was a text from Rowan.

Can't text now. Will try you after work.

So, he still had a job. Not sure why I was so relieved for him, given my present situation and the lack of clarity I had on his marital status.

But he didn't text me after work. And he didn't text me that night. Soon worry turned to anger.

Days dragged by. About a week later, there was a knock at my front door around 8:00 in the morning. I opened the door to find Rowan in his jeans and a flannel shirt. He looked down at the floor as he walked through the door.

And suddenly, I knew. Edith had been right, about that at least.

All the words came tumbling out with fresh tears: "Why didn't you call me? Where have you been? Did you hear what happened to me? Edith says you aren't separated."

"Stop," he soothed, taking my hand.

I twisted away from him, pulling my arm away from his reach.

"Well?" I said with all the tone that would come from that single word.

"I heard what happened to you. This whole thing really scared me. It hit too close to home. I can't jeopardize my job like that. We should take some time apart."

"WHAT?" I think I yelled it, more than said it. "So, you're still married, aren't you? You aren't separated at all?"

He sat on the couch. "I am. Married, I mean. Not separated."

"How? Why did you...?"

Over the next hour he explained it all to me. Slowly. Repeating it when I couldn't follow. He was calm. I imagined how he must be with his kids when they were worked up over something benign. It all came out. The lies about the separation, about having his kids every other weekend, about the apartment that he and his wife "traded off." The lies about why we couldn't be together during the week and why he rarely stayed over. All of it.

Of all the life-altering news I had been handed over the past few days, this was the most devastating. Speechless, I stared at him blankly.

Then he got up and said, "I'll leave. Are you going to be OK?"

I moved toward the front door. I opened it and as he walked toward it and, for reasons I'm still not sure, I hugged him and leaned in. I smelled the familiar smell of his neck and kissed him there. Then I stared at the floor as he walked through the door.

27

The following weeks were a blur, as I attempted to determine my next steps, workwise. I put out feelers for opportunities nearby and did some spring-cleaning in my home, despite it being winter. I stayed busy. I noticed some new texts on my phone one day. I had since given out my new number to all my contacts.

But it was Rowan: *Just checking on you.*

I sighed. Why couldn't I hate him? I blocked his number. Another text from him followed: *I'm sorry.*

I couldn't even block numbers correctly, so I turned off the phone.

A year passed. A new voicemail appeared on my phone. It was early in the morning, and I was just about to back out of my driveway to head to work. The voicemail could wait.

I forgot all about the message until later that evening. It was Rowan. He missed me and wanted to know how I was. He told me to call back only if I wanted. Otherwise, if I didn't, he would understand. He then said, "I wasn't getting a response to all of my texts, so I just wanted to tell you I was sorry."

Yeah, I know. I got that text.

But texts? Plural? What texts?

Google told me where the blocked texts went. I followed Google's instructions. I had successfully blocked his number, after all, because the special section was full of texts from Rowan. One a day for the past three months. Ninety texts.

In the most recent one he wrote, *I promised myself I would give up at day 90. I would let you go.*

I gasped. And I read them. All of them.

Each one was short. They varied. *Drove by the place we had our first date,* or, *The charity BBQ is coming up again,* and, one in the middle of the string was: *Edith was packaged off.* Most were like *I wish you were still in my life,* or, *I want to see you.*

I wasn't sure what to do. There hadn't been a message for three days, and then his voicemail arrived.

I texted him: *Got ur messages, just now. Long story. Hope u r well.*

That night I carried on with my usual routine and was surprised how much I thought about Rowan. But I knew I couldn't go there. Not again. He had already taken so much from me.

28

Except that I wasn't as strong as I'd hoped. Maybe I was flattered, or curious, or, as I'd feared, in love with this married man.

The next day there was no response to my text as I headed out the door to work. It was later in the day when I realized I hadn't unblocked Rowan's number. After unblocking his number I went to the blocked message spot again to restore any that were there. He had responded. With a rush of texts.

Thx 4 responding. How r u? What r u up 2 these dayz? Do u still live on Vine street? R u working? Can I see u?

It was three days later that I texted him a single word: *Yes.*

We saw each other whenever he had scraps of time. It was a hot reconnection, and I heard from him frequently. But he knew, this time around, he didn't need to hide his marital status from me and, good or bad, I started to hear about her, too.

Can't meet up tonight cuz my wife is out with GFs. Or *Would love to chat, but she's here watching TV with me.*

I was not excited about this new transparency. But, eyes wide open, I decided to take it for what it was. I deeply cared about him and repeatedly reminded myself that I wasn't breaking any vows—he was.

Our relationship, if you can call it that, lasted on and off for another fourteen months. It ended, ultimately when we were having a heart-to-heart about his displeasing marriage. I asked him, "Why don't you just leave?" and his response was "I did."

Wait, what? He left her? When?

"About a month after you left the company, after you and I lost touch, I met another woman. She was a parent of one of the kids on my son's football team. She was long divorced, and I moved in with her."

I felt the heat rising up my neck onto my cheeks. He left his wife? For another woman, one he met ONE MONTH after ending it with me? And had MOVED IN with her?

"Stop talking," I said and stood up. "I think sharing time is over."

"Rebekah, please. I'm not with her anymore. Don't be like that. I finally realized what I was doing to my kids, and I moved back home. I'm back with my wife."

Well, I knew he was with his wife. I just thought he was *still* with his wife, not that he had *gone back* to her.

"Why did you come back to me?" I asked, knowing that my original theory that he loved me was false.

"The woman I was seeing gave me an ultimatum and if I went home, she was going to end it," he admitted.

Smart woman. I should've had her give me some of that strength.

"So, I am your consolation prize?" I yelled.

Rowan pleaded, but I remained firm.

"Let me get this straight....you left me in a very vulnerable time in my life, after being a major factor in why I was let go, because you needed space and in that space you found this woman, and you moved into her space and then back to your wife's space to be a better dad. And then, after this woman wised up and kicked your ass to the curb, you thought, I'll text Rebekah. She'll be game."

I was still yelling. But as each word came out, I meant it. I was done. Each time we were together was a lie. What was real for me was apparently not, for him. Understanding that I was "the other woman," I should've had lower expectations for his morals, but I made the mistake of thinking he deeply cared for me.

"Rebekah, I was wrong to let you go. I'm trying to right a wrong."

"You could leave your wife for *her*, but not for me," I countered.

He stood up and said, "Let's just drop this and talk again in the morning. I know I've upset you. But I'm sure you have dated guys since I saw you last."

Which I had. But my heart hadn't been in it. It was still broken.

When he realized I was done, he walked to the door, and I followed silently behind him. He turned to kiss me, and I backed up. His last words to me were, "Sleep well. We can chat more tomorrow."

We didn't chat in the morning. We never chatted again. His texts landed in the blocked section, and it took no willpower to ignore them.

***

About a year after Rowan and I last parted, a friend of mine, whom I had finally divulged the story to months before, texted me: *Did you see the news? The cheater is on the news.*

Sure enough, there he was. Rowan had been let go from the same company where I'd met him.

He was fired for having women back to the warehouse at night and on weekends for romantic trysts. A total of six woman over a period of one year. One of them, scorned at the way he broke up with her, alerted the company, who started surveillance of the warehouse and found out what he was up to. They got names and interviewed the women. He wasn't just fired. He was publicly humiliated. The story stayed in the news for weeks before it died down, and ultimately disappeared.

I never heard what happened to him after that, and frankly I didn't try to find out. But, according to the news reports at the time, he was still with his wife. And they were working on "repairing their relationship."

Well, he did say he was good at repairs.

29

NUMBER FIFTY-SEVEN

I was touring Greece when I met guy number fifty-seven.

Santorini. Paros. Mykonos. Athens. It was on day one of my four days in Mykonos when I met him. Traveling alone, I'd met a couple at my hotel pool, who lived not far from me back home. As is often the case when traveling, bonds form instantly with people who are from your hometown, more so than likely would have, had you met them at home in the first place. After chatting for a bit, I learned they were on their delayed honeymoon.

Balancing their romantic time and their need for the club scene, the couple agreed to accompany me on a bar stroll of the stone-paved streets of Mykonos that evening. We ended up in an overly packed dance club whose booming siren call lured us from the streets. Because it was so crowded, we had to wait at the downstairs bar for our number to be called before we could join the upstairs rave.

While we were waiting downstairs, an attractive, tanned local caught my eye. He was chatting with another guy at a nearby table and glanced at me every so often. He had wavy black hair and was dressed sharply. I told my newfound friend that I liked him. She, perhaps emboldened by the fact that she was on vacation, decided to go over and ask if he was interested in me. I ducked out to the washroom before she reached the table.

When I returned she said, "There you are! I talked to him and he's interested."

And she pointed to the guy next to her. I smiled and nodded at the person standing to her left.

The one I liked was still seated at the table, trying to look busy on his phone.

I yelled in her ear, over the deafening noise, "Wrong guy! It's the other one!" and laughed.

Shocking me, she leaned over to the one beside her and exchanged words. He then left us, returned to the table, and told the other guy something. And then the other guy smiled and got up and approached me. This was too easy, I thought. The only catch was cute guy had no English skills. None. Not one word. He spoke Greek only. And the one I rejected had to serve as his interpreter. It was awkward and hilarious at the same time.

About ten minutes later, our club pager went off, and the honeymooners and I went up the unsteady iron staircase to the dance club. I waved goodbye to "Apollo" on my way up the stairs.

Upstairs, we danced with the music pounding in our ears. The music was so loud the floor was vibrating. And forget about talking. All conversation was lost. After a few dances, we wove our way through the crowd and found the bar, grabbed our complimentary drinks, and returned to the dance area. We laughed at how ridiculous we looked. The floor was so sticky that our flip flops stuck with each step, causing us to stop mid-move, like robots.

About an hour later, the female honeymooner motioned a knife pulling across her neck to signal they were done. She also motioned downstairs, meaning they were leaving. But she put her hands out, indicating "you stay." Which, I did. But only for about another half hour. It was crazy hot in there.

I made my way down the same hazardous staircase we had come up and debated passing through the downstairs bar before heading out. Instead, I decided I would grab a drink in another bar, before joining the lineup for cabs to the outlying hotels.

As I walked past the entrance to the bar, Apollo ran up to me and said "Hello." He pointed to his phone and his Facebook app was open. I nodded and started to spell my name. He shook his head and pointed to my phone and then pointed to himself. I handed him my phone, and he searched for his profile and added it as a contact to my Messenger app.

He leaned in, kissed me on the cheek, and motioned for me to return to the bar. I shook my head and turned to continue my way up the walkway. He nodded and waved. By the time I reached the next bar, he had messaged me, in broken English, asking if I wanted to go to the beach the following day.

He didn't drive, so we met at the beach he suggested. I arrived before him and secured a spot. In Greece, most of the beaches have paid concierge service. For a set fee you get loungers or seats with a table and an umbrella. Some come with food/drink service, but the payment is just for the joy of having a protected location for you and your belongings.

I texted him my location, and he arrived about an hour after me. It was thrilling and unusual all at the same time. We sat in our loungers and applied sunscreen to each other. We jumped in the waves and swam in the ocean. We walked the beach for what seemed like hours, holding hands, playfully splashing each other, stopping to kiss as waves lapped at our feet and calves. It was idyllic. It felt like we were modeling for a swimsuit ad or shooting a commercial for a resort.

Given the language barrier, we didn't talk. To communicate, we motioned and pantomimed. We mimicked drinking or eating or swimming to suggest our next activity. At first it was weird. But after a few hours, we were content with the silence. We realized how little conversation was really needed in our everyday lives. We translated a few things on our phones. I learned his occupation, why he didn't speak English even though it was taught in school, how long he had lived in Mykonos, and where he had traveled.

Whereas, I explained where I lived, where I was traveling next in Greece, and how long I would be in Mykonos. He was very attentive, and there was only a flicker of frustration from time to time as he struggled to communicate.

Around 7:00 p.m. we left the beach and went out for dinner. Back in the same part of Mykonos where he and I first met, his cousin joined us and acted as our interpreter. The evening flowed a lot better than the day, and there was a lot more conversation as a result.

As the night wound down, I knew we would end up back at my resort. Outside guests were not permitted, and they had security cameras in the lobby and pool areas to enforce their policy. I had checked in alone a few days before, and the hotel manager had made a big fuss over giving me the newly remodeled room in the quiet area at the back of the resort. But I knew the same employees were not constantly working and that if we acted like we belonged there, no one would question it.

We walked swiftly past the entrance, reception, and the pool, as we headed toward the back of the resort, which faced a large hill. Although my room had a patio and a hot tub, the hot tub was not working. I was able to mime this to Apollo and he understood.

Once inside we made quick use of the walk-in, multi-nozzle shower enclosure. The walls and floor were crafted entirely from slate, and there were recessed neon lights around the ceiling that allowed you to shower in relative darkness while still casting sufficient light.

In the shower he rubbed soap on my back. At that exact moment, I thought, *I cannot remember the last time someone rubbed soap on my back.* Then I washed his hair. He moaned slightly, and I took this to mean the same as I was thinking.

After showering we dried each other off.

We had not spoken a word since leaving his English-speaking cousin. Instead, we shared gestures and nods. He turned down the bed, and I saw him set the alarm on his phone. At the bedside he took his towel off and flung it on a nearby chair. He had no tan lines. So either it was his natural coloring, or he sunbathed nude. Either way, it was incredibly arousing.

There were a few tattoos on him that I'd seen when we were at the beach. I traced the symbols and foreign words with my fingertips. As I was doing this, he turned and kissed me. He started with my lips, covered my whole face, and moved down my entire body. The kisses and caresses extended all the way to my feet. My body was tingling.

Without words or being able to discuss preferences, he motioned different positions to me, seeking consent. I nodded each time, and we continued to explore each other for hours.

I woke to the sound of the shower, again. I watched him from the bed. He had a towel around his waist. The he pulled on his t-shirt and the towel was off. Next came his boxers and jeans—fashionable jeans that fit him well. He showed me his phone, and I saw a translated text that said: *Hot shower. Hot sex. Beautiful woman.*

I got out of bed and kissed him. I tried to nudge him toward the bed again. He laughed and took my hand and walked me to the front door. He pointed to the lock on the door and made the motion of locking it securely while mumbling in Greek. We kissed again, and I watched him until he rounded the corner of the tall white walls that lined the resort.

After locking up, I went back to bed and slept for another few hours. I woke up to a barrage of texts. Too many really. Texts that asked, in rudimentary English, how I slept. Texts that asked what I was doing that day and where was I going and could we meet for dinner. He asked if I wanted to skip the other islands and stay in Mykonos. And then there were texts about my body, my hair, and the clothes I wore. I read them all but didn't respond. What I'd interpreted as a fun couple of days in a beautiful setting with a wonderful partner, seemed much more to him. Too much more.

Later that day I went scuba diving and then relaxed by the pool and started to plan my Athens adventure, staying close to home to avoid future encounters with Apollo. I have seen Mykonos portrayed in movies since my time there—the idyllic waters with restaurants adorning the shoreline and rocky paths with the well-dressed tourists who tread on them. Each time it brings back memories of my chance Greek encounter—the silent day on the beach and the connection two people can have without even saying a word.

30

NUMBER TWENTY-EIGHT

Guy number twenty-eight was once a good friend of guy number one. I knew him for about five years, as a friend, before we started dating. And he is someone that I have, during our many years apart, escalated to sainthood. Well, sainthood is probably a stretch...but I have created an image of him and how wonderful he was when I dated him that I grapple with why I ever ended our relationship. And I know he's not this too-good-to-be-true guy that I've conjured up, but for some reason my mind has created this fantasy that the grown-up, married, responsible family man he has become was a missed opportunity on my part.

Nowadays, we communicate sporadically, usually with him sending a text asking which country I am in and me responding with some random pic requiring him to guess.

OK, it looks like you are in Europe from the architecture and maybe that church spire suggests Spain or Portugal?

And with each picture I send, he narrows it down until he guesses correctly. Then I give him a four-line update on my life, and he does the same. And our texts go silent for the usual six-month dormant period until one of us reaches out again.

I have never met his wife nor seen any pictures of his children, and despite our well-intentioned "we should get together for a drink" pronouncements, we never do. Part of me thinks it is because of the fictional Wyatt I have dreamed up won't actually compare with the real Wyatt that would be having drinks with me. And part of me thinks my hesitation might be because he has turned out just as awesome as I've pictured, and then I'd feel really crappy for letting a good one slip away.

When we dated, I was more experienced and my "he was my number 28" was counterbalanced by his "I was his number 2." We had great times together. Seeing friends, going to movies, trying new eateries and generally being close. He was very tall (probably still is) and very funny (definitely still is). And our time together was electric.

When we dated, both of us were still living with our parents, and I recall a two-week stint where a friend of my family had asked me to go to their home regularly to check on it in their absence. My duties were pretty generic: Check for break-ins, look for any leaking facets, and turn on/off different lights to give the illusion of the house being inhabited.

On each of these visits Wyatt and I made love on a different piece of furniture. We ran out of furniture to christen before the house-sitting task was complete. And we joked that this prim-and-proper woman would never even guess what had happened on her kitchen table, or bathroom vanity, or basement recliner while she was gone. Wyatt said he had more sex in those two weeks then he'd had in his whole life.

Once we went to a friend's cabin for the weekend. The host thought it was my *friend* Wyatt coming with me, since Wyatt was already known to the group as a friend of guy number one. The host didn't know that Wyatt and I had started dating (epic failure on my part), so we were assigned a room with twin beds. I also recall how a very tall Wyatt and I managed to curve our bodies into a comfortable position while trying to stay on a tiny mattress that squeaked every time we moved. I can still hear us giggling as we tried our best to be quiet.

After an hour or so we gave up trying to get any sleep and snuck out for a not-so-secret nighttime swim in the lake. We napped until morning in a hammock covered in nothing but towels. Suffice it to say, our friend realized we'd kicked our relationship up to the next level when he found us entangled on the hammock the next morning.

You're probably wondering why I ended it with Wyatt. I mean he sounds perfect, right? Well, that's precisely it. He was too nice and too available. Looking back, I'm aghast that I could even think that. It was your classic case of "if I only knew then what I know now." If only my future self could have warned me that nice and available guys were hard to come by.

If only.

Our six-month dating spell, a lifetime when you are in your twenties, ended because I also thought he liked me too much. And I needed space. And although I really enjoyed our time together, I needed time for other things, too. And I thought he should see his friends and not just wait for me to be free.

Instead of vocalizing this like an adult, I just told him I didn't feel the same way for him that I once did. It was a lie. A hurtful one, that I now regret.

Even so, there was no fuss or emotional aftermath. In fact, our lives and groups of friends were separate enough that we didn't even really need to see each other if we didn't want to. And before too long, I was dating someone else and didn't think of Wyatt much. Until decades later, when I started to think about what I had given up and what might have been.

Don't get me wrong. I don't sit around lusting after him, and I'm not even sure that if he suddenly became available that our lives would even comingle well at this point—or if he would even be interested. And I am genuinely happy that he has a family and seems content with his life. The information I get in the brief exchanges suggest he picked the right path.

And when I get those texts that say something like, "Hey Bex.... you got shoes or fins on?"

I smile. I smile because he has reached out. I smile because we were friends first, and it seems we always will be.

And I smile because many of those times I do have fins on.

31

NUMBER SIXTY-THREE

Guy number sixty-three was a complete surprise.

I had gone to a bar's reopening, lured by the reviews of the new décor and great free appetizer platters. The hype included a list of activities like magicians, musicians, and local celebrities that would be in attendance. It was a Tuesday night, a strange day to have a bar reopening, and, from the poor turnout, I wondered if they had made a mistake.

The place was divided into the restaurant side and the bar side. The restaurant portion was quite full, and I spotted the mayor drifting between the crowded tables. The bar side, however, was barren.

From my seat at the bar, I practically had the whole area to myself. While I was hoping for a bigger turnout, I decided that even if the party was a bust, I might as well eat something before heading home. The bartender had yet to greet me.

After about fifteen minutes of sitting alone, I started to wonder if the bar was closed. That was when someone sat on the barstool right next to me. With a whole bar full of empty stools and empty tables, this person sat next to me. It was pretty obvious he'd singled me out. I didn't look up right away, though. Around that time, the bartender clued in and brought over menus and asked, "What can I get you two?"

It was then that I glanced at my new "neighbor" and saw a younger stunning-looking guy, simply dressed, with a nearly shaved haircut and well-defined biceps.

I decided to play along and ordered a pint of beer. He did the same.

Then we each ordered food. We also watched the TV screens, messed with our phones, and made polite conversation about how unbusy it was. The bar population had grown to ten, which still seemed like a paltry amount for a reopening.

We each got a second beer. Around this time I joked with guy sixty-three that the bartender probably had us on the same check, and I thanked him for picking up the tab when it came. We reached the point in our conversation where we shared what brought us to the bar. I was hoping to see some friends from town at the reopening; whereas, he was in town on business teaching tactical drills to fire recruits and had no idea of the reopening. He had simply come for dinner.

Our banter took us through beer number two. I came out of the washroom shortly thereafter and saw him paying our check. I had told him about another bar he should hit in town if he wanted a livelier scene. As I walked up, he said he was off to "Brews." To avoid seem-ing overly interested (which I was!), I sat down to finish the remainder of my pint as he got up and put his jacket on. I was planning on leaving after my beer, but I didn't want to get up until he was gone.

And that's when I noticed out of the corner of my eye that it was taking him a long time to find whatever was in his jacket pocket. He even pulled out his barstool and looked at the ground. After a few minutes I decided to break the awkward silence with what I thought to be an obvious question.

"Drop something?" I asked, taking the last sip of my beer and looking for the bartender so I could settle up.

"Nope," he mumbled. "Just waiting."

"Waiting?" I asked, somewhat confused.

"Waiting for you to finish your drink so we can go to Brews."

Wow. I'd thought for a second there I'd misread him.

Trying my best to sound nonchalant, I responded, "OK, let me just grab my check."

Before I could signal the bartender, he smiled: "Got it already. Remember?"

"Nice," I said trying not to blush as we left.

Neither of us had driven, so we walked the relatively short distance to Brews, chatting comfortably. We talked about our jobs, where he lived, and how the next day was going to be an early start for him since training started at six in the morning. He groaned when he heard my freelance job allowed me to work from home and how I'd planned to offset the late night by sleeping in.

When we got to Brews we grabbed a table, as if it were an everyday occurrence. I went to the bar, grabbed beers for both of us, and asked if he wanted to move to the bar to be with the crowd instead of sitting at the table. He nodded and picked up his beer, and we relocated to the boisterous bar rail.

At the bar we talked with the other patrons and gave song requests to the bartender to play on the sound system. Some of the choices were questionable, which caused some of us to laugh. Soon the whole row of us were calling out the next song that should be played. There were definite sparks between Joshua and me. At one point, after a return from one of our trips to the washroom, our barstools got closer together, and our legs were touching. Soon after, we were looking at pictures on each other's phones.

Our talking got a lot more intense, too. He told me he used to be a stripper before he became a firefighter, and now he was a trainer for the new recruits. His pictures just blew me away. Every inch of him was chiseled perfection.

When he used "we" when referring to something at home, I sat up straighter. *We?* I didn't like the sound of that, and he noticed. But we continued our discussions and our banter, but my mind shifted from "Look what I found!" to "I wonder where she thinks he is?"

Our mutual attraction was obvious, and I did my best to hide my disappointment at his new disclosure about his wife and their life together. Still, we had a good time, and I didn't let the fact that I'd read the situation wrong change my mood.

And then, when we least expected it, the bar was closing. In a small town, during the week, closing time was discretionary. Since the night was coming to an unexpected end, I settled my tab and ordered a cab knowing the wait time would be unpredictable, given it was 11:00 p.m. on a Tuesday.

Joshua had stopped at the storefront of Brews before last call and purchased a six-pack for the following day to enjoy after his training. When I heard him ask the bartender how to get a cab back to the training camp, the bartender and I both told him there was only one cab in town, and he would have to catch the one I was taking after it had dropped me off.

Joshua laughed and said, "Where am I? I didn't think I was *that* far from civilization."

I chuckled: "You'll be lucky if the cab even comes back for you. You might be better off calling one of the other firefighters to come and get you."

Without giving his ride back another thought, I said goodnight and headed outside to wait for my taxi in the night air. There was some snow on the ground, but it was a surprisingly mild night. Soon after, Joshua walked out of the bar and stood with me. He was on the phone with someone. I found it intriguing that he didn't walk away to make the call. He made it right next to me. I could tell from the conversation that it wasn't a firefighter he was speaking to. And he wasn't asking for a ride. It sounded like he was talking to his wife. I heard a recount of his evening. Then he described meeting me and shared a few things about the conversations we had and how he was waiting for his cab with me. I heard him say he had six beers "to go" and that he was hoping to have a hot tub later.

The fireman training center has a hot tub? Noice!

My phone rang and jolted me from my thoughts. It was the cab driver, letting me know he'd just dropped someone off and was about ten minutes away. He wanted to know if I still needed him, and I said yes.

Joshua saw me hang up. And then said, "I don't want the night to end. Do you?"

"Well, the last bar just closed, so unless we're going to split that six-pack in the parking lot, I think it is," I said, laughing.

"What about a hot tub? You said you had a hot tub, right?"

"Yes, but you said you had a wife," I said matter-of-factly.

"Well, here's the thing. She won't mind. Just ask her."

Stunned, I stared back at him. He handed me his phone, which still had the time ticking from his call, a call that he'd never hung up from. So, she had just heard our discussion. The one where Joshua asked to come to *my* place.

Holding his phone, I noticed the display said *Wife*. On the screen there was a picture of a petite blond with model-quality features. I stared back at it, frozen, unsure of what I should do.

And then I heard, "Hello?" from a female voice.

Was he serious? His wife, his wife wants to talk to me?

"Hello?!?!?" I heard again, a little louder from the speaker.

"Hello?" I asked, confused.

"Is that you, Rebekah? Joshua said you guys were having a great time tonight. That is until the bar closed."

I thought if this was a friend of his, pretending to be his wife, he went through a lot of effort to set up this charade and put the contact in his phone under *Wife*.

"Yes, it was fun, but I'm headed home now. Here's your husband." And I pushed the phone back in his hand.

Still on speaker he said, "Hey, Lore."

Was that short for Lori?

"I told Rebekah you wouldn't mind if I went to her place for a hot tub. She doesn't seem to believe me. Can you help me out?"

"Nope, you go ahead, have fun." Lore said from the speaker.

"What?" I cried, now laughing.

"And Rebekah, if you are game, we can do more than just have a hot tub. Your call." Joshua said his words into the phone but looked directly at me.

I covered my mouth, expecting the wife, or friend, to laugh or yell.

And to my surprise Lore said, "Sure, he's all yours. But just for tonight, OK? He's just on loan."

And without hesitation, I quipped, "Oh, like a library book."

And she said, "Yep, you guys have fun. Josh, call me tomorrow. Damn, if I was there, I would join you guys."

What?

Suddenly I was aware that the cab, the town's only cab, would be here soon and a decision would need to be made.

After the call ended, Joshua asked me what I thought....did I want company?

Hell yes.

Not only because he was fit, fun, and very eager, but also because this was the wildest scenario I had ever encountered. Permission from someone's wife to sleep with her husband: a chiseled firefighter/former stripper. I mean, how could I turn that down?

I asked him to pull up his Facebook profile and show me his relationship status. He did, and the status was blank. But then he clicked on her profile, and I saw a Lori with the same last name as his. They were around the same age. Her profile had many pics of them as a couple, posing in ways that would be unlikely for a sister, or other relative with the same last name.

When the cab arrived we both got in as I called out my address to the driver.

While we were in the car, I asked, "The first bar was dead. There were so many seats, even at the bar. Why did you sit right next to me?"

He grinned at me and said, "Because when I walked in and saw you, I thought...what are the odds I come to this small-ass town and find a great-looking girl sitting all by herself?"

And here I was thinking I was the lucky one...

32

The hot tub was a delicious experience.

Joshua was outside soaking already in his boxers, with a beer in hand, when I appeared in the doorway with just a white tank top on. I wasn't sure of the dress code for the event. And I knew he didn't have bathing trunks, so I gambled.

We shared the beer and listened to the playlist I had put on the overhead speakers. It didn't take long for him to remove his boxers and toss them over the side of the tub. I watched as they landed in the snow. Having a secluded backyard definitely has its perks.

I grinned as he pulled off my tank top and tossed it over the side of the tub into the snow.

We indulged in this alternate-life fantasy for some time. Then we turned off the hot tub and went inside. I was surprised when he asked to stay over, but then I remembered the cab situation prevented his leaving anyhow.

We got ready for bed in the bathroom at the double sinks. I laughed with my mouth full of toothpaste when he winked at me in the mirror, both of us naked.

***

The next morning I woke to a kiss on my forehead.

"It was great meeting you."

"What time is it?" I groaned.

"It's early. Go back to sleep."

I did fall back to sleep. And when I woke up, he was gone. There was just a note in the kitchen with the last full can of beer on top of it. The note read: *Cheers, Josh.*

When I was fully awake, I Googled his name and his so-called wife's name. I found out that Lori was indeed his wife. His whole story was true right down to where he worked and where he lived.

I found it was altogether an unbelievable, yet special, evening. I guess it was possible to go out for a bar reopening and end up having your own eyes opened.

I also found out that the world was full of surprises.

But what I didn't find was my white tank top … not until spring.

33

NUMBER NINETEEN

Guy number nineteen and I in were in love, but neither one of us would admit it. Looking back, I think that was probably for the best.

Grant and I met while I was spending a year in Thailand. He was living there full-time, working at his parents' hotel. They owned three hotels in the beachside towns, and the chain was well known to the budget-minded traveler. A *hotel* might be a bit of an overstatement. The rooms were more like a college dorm: simple units with a bed or two, a desk, and a small fridge. There were two common cooking areas, two common TV lounge areas, shower/washroom facilities, and coin-operated washing machines. From the air, the building resembled a "V" and regardless of what room you lived in, you passed through your common kitchen and lounge on your way in or out of the building.

At the center of the "V" was a garden, a swimming pool, and a BBQ area, complete with picnic tables, lights strung in the trees, and an outdoor movie screen. A large fence separated the property from its nearby neighbors, and along the fence was a clothesline for tenant use. At the top of the "V," but not attached, was a lovely bungalow with many trees surrounding it. That was the home where Grant and his family lived.

The owners enjoyed having young people stay, offering them a haven during their travels, where longer-term stays were encouraged. In addition to paying rent, guests were expected to complete some sort of helpful chore each week, on rotation. It was also well-known that Grant's parents offered more chores in lieu of full rent for those travelers who were not flush with cash.

Local bulletin boards displayed ads for paying jobs in the nearby towns, and there was other signage about rideshare programs to get to and from the worksites. There was very little public transit in the immediate area, and no one owned a car or had enough money to take a taxi regularly. Grant's parents also offered rides to various places if they were going anyway, so it was not on a regular schedule. In short, his parents treated us twenty-somethings like one of their own kids; same behavior expectations and you gave them respect in return.

Grant worked the front desk, as did his sister Malee, on occasion. His family was from England and had opened the hotels after Grant's father found accommodations limited on a business trip to Thailand over a decade before. Fourteen years later, the family joked that it was the longest trial basis ever.

I spent three stints at their home-away-from-home, aptly named "Our Place." My first stay was for one week that turned into two months.

I checked in with a friend, Kate. She and I had met earlier that week, on the beach, while learning to surf—or attempting to anyhow. Both of us had been in the country for over a month, and we had tentative plans to move on together to another part of Thailand at the end of the week.

Neither of us kept those plans.

We met Grant's dad and sister when we checked in and the handful of times one of us went to ask questions. I didn't meet Grant until two days before I was scheduled to move on. His family was hosting a BBQ in the courtyard. Kate and I had seen the flyer, and we were excited at the chance to meet new people. Kate was looking to sell some of her extra gear, and I was hoping to find travel companions for the next leg of our trip.

Grant was trying to figure out the faulty wiring in the outside speaker system when Kate and I arrived. I offered to help the person with his back to me, crouched over the power box. He called out a few instructions, and I ran to jiggle the wires at the speakers, as requested. After a few attempts, the music was blaring, and the group cheered.

Grant, whom I finally saw face-to-face, said, "Thanks, Rebekah."

He already knew my name. You'd think I would have been thrown by that. But actually, I was kind of intrigued.

"And you are?"

"Grant. My dad said you and Kate are leaving us in a couple of days."

"Yes, we're off to Koh Samui. Have you been?"

"Never. Have been meaning to go. You will have to tell me all about it."

Throughout the evening we chatted, between his host duties. Grant was tall, broad-shouldered with surfer-blond hair and a distinctive scar near his lip. He was dressed in mismatched clothes: a pair of plaid shorts and a striped shirt, neither in the same color palette. He was not the type of guy I would be interested in—not the headliner of the party, so to speak—so, it surprised me when I realized I was so drawn to him.

Later in the evening, after the sun set, someone turned off the stereo and brought out their guitar. Soon after, there were two guitars, and some in the group sang along: showtunes, old favorites, and even Christmas carols, despite the fact we were smack dab in the middle of summer.

Grant and I sat on the end of separate benches. There were a handful of people between us. Each time I looked over at Grant, our eyes met. Funny how we never ended up seated next to one another, but each time one of us got up, we grabbed a refill for the other person, locating the same type of drink in the icy cooler. Then we'd hand it to each other seamlessly, as our previous drink finished, as if we had been reading each other's thoughts for years. If anyone noticed, they didn't say anything.

The next day was quiet. It was the last full day at the hotel for Kate and me. We decided to have a leisurely day and swam, read, borrowed bikes to get lunch for the group, and played a game of volleyball on the hotel's lawn. The teams were not evenly matched talentwise, and people started dropping out until it was three-on-three. Kate was one of the surviving players. I was a player-turned-cheerleader and then slinked back to the pool when a scoring dispute got a little intense. Grant was taking a swim, so I decided to stay.

His tanned arms crested the water and his head alternated from side to side with each breath. I settled into a sun lounger, unnoticed. When I no longer heard the sound of freestyle laps, I looked around and saw Grant drying off at the far end of the pool.

"Last day?" he asked quizzically.

"I guess," I answered, suddenly noncommittal to my impending travel plans.

"Well, I never really got to know you, but I'm glad to have met you. Please come back again, if your agenda permits."

So formal. I wondered if he was just being polite or if maybe he felt something, too, but didn't want to make me uncomfortable. Or maybe he was just honoring hotel policy.

Before I could continue reflecting on the situation, he added, "I was going to go to the wharf for dinner tonight. There are a few bands playing. Did you want to join me?"

I noticed that he said join *me*, not join *us*. Not with his family. Not with his sister. Join him. Just him. I had to find Kate and tell her. When I went to the volleyball court, there was no one there. Then I went to our room, and she wasn't there either. I asked around, and no one had seen her. So, I wrote her a quick note and left it in the room. For good measure, I put another note near the TV in the common room that directed her to the note in our room. I invited her to join us if she didn't have other plans. I wasn't about to abandon my travel partner. If she wanted company that night, she was more than welcome. I've always adhered to the girl code and wasn't going to abandon my "sister" for some "mister."

The evening with Grant was wonderful. We strolled on the boardwalk and walked barefoot in the sand. We watched the sunset from a rock on the shore. We even heard the bands from our vantage point by the shore. It couldn't have been more romantic. We bought dinner and ate out of cardboard containers. The meal was exquisite: meat kebabs, steamed vegetables, and spicy shrimp. It was like we'd been dating for months, each chewing off the other's wood skewer. We also drank curiously strong fruit punch as we sat together, enjoying the moment, our moment.

We talked about his life, including his choice to accompany his parents to Thailand and his decision to stay. I joked that he must have a great dating life, given he meets single women all the time in his line of work. He didn't deny it. But he also said it was a great lifestyle for short-term fun, but it lacked the opportunity for long-term love.

His words hung sweetly in the air, and we both paused, letting them sink in. And then we addressed the obvious: I was no different. I was in transit and was not there for long-term love. And then we laughed, agreeing not to fall in love with each other. We were so determined that we shook on it, still laughing.

Noting the chill in the air, I stood up after the sun had fully set. Grant put his arm around my shoulders. We moved toward the stage. The last band was playing, and the wharf was abuzz with foot traffic. We stepped aside to let a string of cyclists pass by, and then we stopped. I looked up at him, and he smiled tenderly at me. He had one of those smiles that could make you melt. While melting, he took my face in both of his hands and kissed me. I've kissed a lot of men, but Grant was different, and I think he felt it, too.

An hour later we chose to walk back to the hotel. A warm rain was falling. When we parted, more to convince myself than lighten the mood, I said, "Remember our agreement." And he saluted me, as if to say, "Yes ma'am," while flashing that warm smile. That smile made me want to stay. I shook myself back to reality and returned to my room.

Still no Kate. The note was gone, but she wasn't there. And she had not left a note in return. The whole situation was peculiar: me wanting to stay, Kate already gone.

Grant was with me while I was processing Kate's absence. He was puzzled as well and went to see if his parents knew anything. I pulled out my luggage and opened it up on the bed. I might as well start packing.

Grant found me about a half hour later in my room. My door was still open, as was my bag. I had barely made a dent in my packing. I kept reliving the conversations between Grant and me. And our kiss. Our wonderful kiss...

"Kate left," Grant said breathlessly as he walked back into the room.

"For the wharf?" I asked.

"No, like, left the hotel. She's gone."

"What?"

"She checked out."

I was stunned.

That was when I noticed her side of the room was a little barer. When I opened her closet all that was left were the dresses and gear she had been trying to sell.

But there was no note.

I was baffled. And truth be told, a little pissed off.

34

After learning that Kate had bailed on me, I took my bag, still mostly empty, off the bed and set it aside. I looked Grant right in the eye, testing him. "Want to go for a swim?"

According to the rules, after-hours swims were not permitted. Given the pool's location, the noise echoed could wake those in the nearby rooms. I was sure Grant would say no or give me an excuse about the pool chemicals or his parents. Instead, he nodded and took my hand as we crept down the back staircase to the hut behind the pool. He dimmed the pool's lights—both the ones on the patio and the ones inside the pool. But he left the waterfall on.

We slipped out of our clothes, quietly descended the pool steps, and waded into the chest-deep water. We floated down to the rock waterfall and kissed. Then we drifted together, staring up at the sky. But we did not make love. It was very sensual just to be naked and so close to him, even without the sex.

When we got out of the pool, he kissed me just before he adjusted the pool lights and whispered, "Don't worry about Kate. Maybe you can stay a few extra days while you sort out your plan?"

And I stayed for an extra few days. An extra fifty-three days...

During those two months, Grant and I discovered Thailand and each other. Despite having lived there for many years, Grant had ventured sparingly beyond his family's hotels. He had traveled extensively throughout neighboring countries but said he never seemed to find time to discover the nearby beaches or take touristy day trips.

We made the most of our time together. We sailed on the sea. We played in the pool. We ate at local markets. Grant read me poetry and turned me on to foreign films. And, in return, he endured a weekly reality TV show, my shameless obsession at the time.

We referred to each other as boyfriend and girlfriend, despite my known departure. We were pragmatic and didn't pretend as if the day wouldn't come. To keep our agreement, we reminded ourselves that we were not in love. Some days, though, the words were just a whisper.

For my birthday he took me on a small plane to an island. We were the only ones on the plane—and the island. It was an impromptu scuba trip, followed by champagne and a sunset. I felt like the richest person in the world. The crew on the boat thought we were getting engaged. We smiled and pretended that we were. It was a fun moment. But, the whole time, I knew it was going to come to an end.

After two months had passed, we had a farewell BBQ in the yard. And when I left, I traveled to Koh Tao for a planned adventure working and living on a dive yacht. The job provided compensation in the form of floating accommodation, fish-friendly food, and unlimited diving.

In exchange, I helped on the boat, assisted the paying passengers, and slept in a berth with three other crew members.

After a few weeks, I craved life on the shore. I enjoyed my yacht life, but I was wanting to exchange my sea legs for land legs. I disembarked on another island that served as my home for the next month.

Grant and I had agreed not to contact each other after we parted. We knew that our lives would continue. Our goodbye hadn't been dramatic. It had been touching. He said "thank you" and that my arrival showed him that perhaps he wanted something beyond the hotel business, but he also acknowledged his tie to helping his parents—perhaps at the expense of his own pursuits. We never discussed him joining me. We both knew what we had, whatever it was, would end at some point anyhow.

After a month on the Thai island of Koh Chang, I broke my word and returned to Our Place.

Grant was out that day. I checked in and headed out to nab some groceries. I had told Grant's mother, in the front office, that my stay was for two weeks. She seemed thrown by my return. I was unsure if the displeasure was the unexpected nature of my arrival, its two-week duration, or my presence entirely.

Grant, however, felt differently. We picked up where we had left off. In that time, he thankfully hadn't (a) left the hotel, (b) found his soul mate, or (c) lost his feelings for me. I enjoyed our reconnection, as did he.

My second departure was harder.

This time we saw what our rekindling did to each other. We were frustrated with the situation, not with each other or our needs independent of each other. It was the quirk of fate that put us together in different stages of our lives, residing in different countries that was hard to accept.

We spent the entire twenty-four hours before my flight as a unit. People gave us space.

His mom came to me and told me that she wanted me to be happy. But she also said she wanted me to go: "There is no future for you two. You are a distraction to Grant."

I told Grant what she said. Wisely, he said she had a point. While I knew they were both right, there were tears at the airport. More of mine, than his.

Good thing we weren't in love.

Aside from Grant, my trip to Indonesia was a great diversion and ultimately my favorite part of my year away. I indulged in a laid-back, nomadic lifestyle, one that I have yet to repeat. I had no time limits on my stay, other than my return to the States three months later. I could add other islands or spend all my time in heaven on earth. My choices were my own.

During my trip, I woke each day with no agenda and retired each night feeling calm and at peace. As my return to real life approached, I reflected on my eleven months away. And broke my word. Again.

Without advance warning, I turned up at Grant's hotel one last time. I hesitated before walking up the lane, worried about what I might find. Although gone a few months, I had not forgotten Grant's mother's words. Or Grant's sobering affirmation of them. I almost turned around and headed away, when I saw him through the front window, standing in the front office, talking to a woman. He was gesturing animatedly with his hands. I was unsure from my vantage point whether she was a guest or perhaps someone special in his life.

Was it worth the risk to sour our time together by trying to squeeze out a few more weeks?

I decided to take a risk and walked up the lane.

35

There were two guests checking in. I set down my overstuffed backpack and waited my turn, taking care to avoid eye contact. The woman, whom I had misunderstood to be a guest or a girlfriend from a distance, was actually an employee. She assisted with a couple's check-in, leaving Grant free to look my way.

At first, I wasn't sure he recognized me. I hadn't changed much, but his eyes didn't register initially. Or so it seemed. Then he walked around the desk, headed toward me without a word, and gave me a rib-crushing hug. He held me so tight, I could barely breathe, and then he cradled my head gently in his hands, and we kissed.

I cried. Not a blubbery cry or a bang-your-elbow kind of cry. It was more a cry of relief. I had missed him. This time Our Place felt like *our place*. Grant's parents and Malee had moved back to England for an undetermined period of time to deal with a health scare of another family member. This left Grant running the show, with newly hired help.

Eager to pitch in, I moved into the main house and helped with the BBQ events and shuttled guests to town. Grant and I did everything together: ate in restaurants, held hands, swam in the ocean, tanned on the beach, and surfed.

A week before my ultimate departure from Thailand, Kate returned! Forgiveness is easy when you are young. We made up for lost time by picking up as if she had never left. I updated her on my relationship with Grant. We obsessed over it and dissected it, as only women can do.

We lived in the moment. Kate and me. Me and Grant. And just me. But as sure as rain fell in summer afternoons and tides shifted, the day to leave came.

Kate, now staying, hugged me goodbye in the lane—our rift forgotten, our lives forever entwined. Grant got in the jeep to drive me to the airport. Without doors and a roof, the most obvious object in the car was my backpack. It spoke volumes. On the ride we hardly spoke. I think it was because it was easier to just leave things unsaid.

When we arrived, Grant pulled the jeep into the loading zone with the flashers on. We pulled my oversized bag from its spot, dropping it heavily on the pavement. We laughed awkwardly, as if some of our closeness had already escaped us.

I spoke first.

"Grant...I want to thank..."

"Please don't—" he interjected. "There is nothing I want to hear that will make this not what it is."

I couldn't disagree.

I wished that this was one of those false starts, one of those other times I had left and where I ended up back in his arms. But we both knew this was it. The finish line.

He walked me to the check-in area, leaving the traffic conductor whistling in distress at the vehicle parked in the loading zone. After my bag was whisked away and I was left with a boarding pass showing my assigned seat, I turned to him and said, "Remember our agreement?"

"Not to fall in love," he responded.

"Good thing we didn't break that," I said, sniffling.

Grant, careful to guard his feelings, simply said, "Take care, Rebekah. Man, please take care."

And then there was the hug. That hug was crushing. Not in strength, but in meaning. I pulled away and kissed him. On the lips. For a long time. Long after he tried to wrench free, embarrassed by our scene.

It was hard to walk away, but eventually I let go and caught my flight. While I never returned, we did stay in touch. We followed each other's lives on social media. We even saw each other again when he came to visit me in the States. But it wasn't the same. He seemed colder somehow—older, worn down.

I saw his Facebook posts about his marriage, the birth of his daughters, his divorce, and his next marriage. He also posted about the death of his parents and his subsequent move out of Thailand.

We had a few in-depth chats on social media. But mostly they were just "likes" and comedic comments on each other's posts. Nothing that would suggest what we might have been once to each other. Because, after all, we were never in love...

36

NUMBER FIFTY-FIVE

I met guy number fifty-five at a networking event during an out-of-town-conference. It was your typical end-of-day event that you'd expect at a weeklong convention: hot appetizers on trays, drab nonalcoholic punch, and a line at the cash bar. The room was filled with participants, some in business attire and others in jeans.

What struck me as odd were the six or so people who were lined up to shake some guy's hand and pose for a photo with him. He hadn't been a speaker at that day's conference, and I didn't recognize his picture from the next day's program. So, I had no clue who he was. Most of the people in my assigned group, however, seemed to know his name, Albert-something, and one of them proudly showed a picture of the two of them, captured on his phone.

People ebbed and flowed from the circle where I was standing, and the topics of discussion ranged from cooking habits and workplace woes to home renovations. It seemed everyone had a home-renovating story to share. We talked about the current TV hits and popular hosts of reality shows. I saw when the fans around Albert dissipated and he, with his male colleague, moved toward the bar line. The other people in line ahead of him, parted for him, or so it seemed from my vantage. By now, however, I was too embarrassed to ask, *again*, who this Albert-guy was.

I had just managed to free myself from a new group of uninteresting nonstop talkers when Albert and his colleague walked over to where I was standing. We introduced ourselves (first names only) and kept the conversation light, mostly talking about the weather and the conference. Albert also asked me a few questions, showing interest in my answers.

There was an uncomfortable lull in the conversation that Albert seemed to handle better than I did. After a moment, Albert shared that his colleague, whom he referred to as "his assistant," had gone to make an inquiry about an amenity that had not been provided in Albert's room.

The hotel was luxurious, and it came as no surprise to me that many conference attendees were staying off-site at more modest accommodations. I had maxed out the allowable expense my company had provided and booked a room at the hotel. And I was loving it. I think I may have gushed a little too much to Albert, in hindsight, about my great room and asked if his was the same.

"It sounds lovely. Mine is...similar," he said after a brief pause.

We talked a bit longer. I drummed up some innocuous conversations, steering away from all things political, religious, or controversial. I figured entertainment was safe, so I asked if he'd seen the most recent blockbuster hit, to which he responded, "I don't get to see many movies, I'm sorry to say."

Since movies were out, I asked about TV shows. Unfortunately, Albert had only seen some shows that I was unfamiliar with. When I asked about travel, he said when he did travel it was for business and he was usually stuck inside all day.

I was running out of things to say, and there was another awkward pause in the conversation. Albert's assistant still hadn't returned, so he offered to refresh my drink. I declined. Soon after, someone joined us and began fiercely pumping Albert's hand and saying, "Great to meet you."

I took advantage of the opportunity to excuse myself and slip away. As the networking event concluded, a few of us decided to extend the evening by venturing to a bar up the street. I was putting on my coat and fastening its multiple buttons when Albert approached me, flanked by his assistant, and asked if they could accompany the group.

"The more the merrier," someone said.

On the short walk, Albert stuck by my side and even lent an arm when we navigated an icy patch on the sidewalk. I had fallen behind the group a little, thanks to my high heels, but I knew the destination wasn't far.

Determined to avoid another uncomfortable lull, I asked, "So, Albert, what do you do for a living?"

His assistant laughed softly when Albert told me he was a cabinetmaker. Now the group's home renovation conversation made sense, and I wondered if perhaps Albert was on one of those shows we had been talking about. Maybe that was why everyone knew him.

Not wanting to seem like I didn't know him, but also trying to keep it real, I said, "Good for you. I mean it's nice to follow your dream and still do something with purpose."

I thought about asking him about kitchen cabinetry, but I figured he likely didn't want to talk about work on a night off, so I refrained.

When we got to the bar, the group grabbed a large table in the noisy bar area. Albert sat near me, and we each engaged in discussions with various people at the table. A couple of men asked Albert questions about the latest political campaign, and I excused myself to the ladies' room. Politics wasn't my type of conversation. I was usually undereducated on the subject and honestly not that interested.

When I returned, the topic had shifted to a recent celebrity scandal and the fallout that surrounded it. Most had heard of it. Albert had not.

Over the next couple of hours, the crowd thinned. And two women at the table scooted closer to Albert and probed him about his family life and his hobbies. I felt I was intruding a bit on their pursuit and on my next trip away from the table, I returned to a different seat on the opposite side and struck up a conversation with Albert's colleague.

At the end of the evening, we settled our tabs and walked back to the hotel as a smaller group. We gathered on the elevator and pressed various floors to our rooms. There were five of us on the elevator. The two ladies who showed interest in Albert, Albert, his assistant, and me. I exited first on the ninth floor and waved goodnight.

Once in my room, I hastily kicked off my shoes, showered, and changed into comfortable clothes and fuzzy socks, noting that it was about 10:00 p.m. I scanned the onscreen guide of TV channels and debated calling room service for a late-night snack when there was a soft knock on my hotel room door. So soft in fact, I thought it might have been the TV. Curious, I walked over in my comfy clothes to peer through the peephole.

It was Albert's assistant.

How did Albert's assistant, the one whom I'd had the briefest of conversations with, know my room number? And what was he doing here? Had he misinterpreted things when I sat beside him at the bar?

I debated ignoring the knock, but my curiosity got the better of me, and I opened the door about a foot.

"Hi," I said, suddenly wondering if ignoring the knock might have been better, given my attire.

"Good evening, Miss Stewart. I hope you were not woken by me."

I was a bit taken aback. *When had I shared my last name?* And then I realized it was probably on the attendee list for the conference.

Still a little uncomfortable with the situation, I said, "No...," and waited for him to continue while taking care to keep the door only slightly ajar.

"Mr. Albert wonders if you might accompany him by sitting for a drink or even a cup of tea in the lobby."

Why was Albert, or "Mr. Albert," not with one of the two women who were fawning over him, and why was his assistant asking on Albert's behalf?

"Tonight?" I asked, surprised.

"If you please," was his answer.

Simultaneously confused and intrigued, I nodded: "OK, but I have to change. I will see you both down there in a bit."

I closed the door when he nodded and turned away and stood there for a moment, processing what had just transpired.

As I entered the hotel bar, I spotted Albert. He was near the fireplace, in a high-back chair. When I got closer, I noticed the fireplace was the electric type that had a fake flame over logs that never changed, but still offered some heat. The adjacent chair was empty and a glass of what appeared to be bourbon or scotch was on a small table beside him. He was reviewing some documents and making rapid marks on them in a red pen as I walked up.

"Rebekah!" he said, partly surprised but mostly pleased. He dropped the documents onto the table turning them over, creating a makeshift coaster for his drink.

I ordered a drink and confessed my ill-timed hunger. We shared a sandwich and talked, this time with remarkable ease. He told me about his aging parents and the feelings of being pulled in many directions, given his work demands and his grown children. His wife had passed away two years prior from a terminal illness, and it sounded like he had not fully come to terms with it.

After the table had been cleared, I asked how he knew my room number and where his assistant had gone.

Albert smiled. "He's very resourceful. I hope you didn't mind."

I stared back at him, waiting for him to elaborate, but it seemed that was the only answer I was going to get.

Close to midnight, someone from the front desk came and whispered in Albert's ear. He excused himself to take a call on the lobby phone. I stood up when Albert did, assuming the evening was over.

Albert smiled: "Do you have to leave? I would love to spend more time together, if you don't mind waiting while I take care of this."

I nodded and ordered a sparkling water and waited by the fake fire. A few minutes later the sparkling water arrived, with Albert in tow.

"I'm sorry to do this, but I need to jump on a conference call. If you don't find it too presumptuous, would you like to come upstairs while I take the call? The documents I need are up there."

What kind of documents does a cabinetmaker need at midnight on a Thursday?

Despite my suspicions, I agreed, and we rode the elevator to the penthouse. It was a spacious suite that made my room look modest in comparison. The adjoining neighbor was his assistant—who reappeared once I was in the suite, poured my sparkling water into a crystal glass, handed me the TV remote, and offered to adjust the room temperature to my liking. I didn't see Albert but could vaguely hear him in the office portion of the suite as I enjoyed the view from the top of the hotel. The city looked so pretty at night. Or was it morning?

Twenty minutes ticked by. I used the decadent washroom with the gold faucets and embroidered towels. As I wiped my hands I wondered if I should leave.

Soon after, Albert reappeared, whispered instructions to his assistant, who then exited into his own suite next door. Albert apologized for his call. He said he'd been trying to reach a group of people all week and that sometimes work couldn't wait.

He cleared the glasses off the coffee table and moved them to the nearby dining area. Then he changed the TV station to music and reached for my hand.

"Dance?"

A dancing cabinetmaker? Who knew?

Dancing is not my forte. I tried to move appropriately and finally gave up, allowing him to sway me as needed to the music. The lights were dimmed, and the city lights sparkled below. It was simultaneously arousing and peaceful.

Then he kissed me, and I kissed him back. He nodded to the adjacent bedroom, and I smiled.

***

The next morning I woke up before him. I slipped out of bed, gathered my clothes, and quietly readied myself in the bathroom. Although I could still make the day's lectures in plenty of time, I had lost interest.

Albert called out, "Leaving?"

"Yes. Thank you for last night. Your room is incredible."

"*You* are incredible," he quipped.

I leaned down over him, still in the bed, and we kissed. And then there was a knock at the main door to the suite.

"Well, it seems my day is underway anyhow," he said, standing and pulling on his boxers.

"Will I see you later? My flight is not until 4:00," he inquired as he put on a pair of jeans and golf shirt that were folded neatly on a nearby chair.

"I don't think I'm staying. I might get an early start on the drive."

"Please call me. I'm in town a lot and would love to see you again," he said.

Albert handed me his business card. I smiled and closed my hand around it, holding my cell phone in the other. I kissed him on the cheek, and his assistant entered the suite and motioned for Albert to join him at the table. Then three other people filed into the room.

Albert waved to me as he took a seat at the dining room table, taking a sip from the coffee cup now in front of him.

Back in my room, I looked at his business card, and then I Googled him.

Albert was not a cabinetmaker. He was a Cabinet *Minister*.

Thankfully I hadn't asked him about my kitchen.

37

NUMBER TWENTY-TWO

Guy number twenty-two met me on a trip where we had a brief encounter and then parted ways. To my surprise, he resurfaced on the next three stops on my journey. When I told my friends about the situation, I emphasized that he met me and not the other way around, because he had orchestrated our encounter.

Billy had seen me at a local market one morning, followed me, at a distance, to my hotel, and then inserted himself into my life. He had secured a room at the same hotel, joined me and my group of my friends around the pool, fished for an invitation to accompany us on our next meal, and our next outing. He was lively, our age, and a fellow traveler. We happily included him.

About two weeks later, my friends and I were leaving, heading west, and Billy was heading south. All of us had a great farewell party around the pool. Billy and I had what I would refer to as "goodbye sex" in a feverish way, knowing we wouldn't be in this beautiful tranquil place again. Or see each other again. I wasn't in love. I wasn't even in overwhelming "like." It was just a fun time, and it was ending.

Or so I thought.

The next day my group and I boarded our bus, and Billy waved to us as it pulled away. And when we arrived at our next destination and dragged our luggage into the hotel, exhausted, who was in the lobby but "goodbye-boy."

My friend said, "Isn't that Billy?" And my jaw dropped.

"My plans changed!" he exclaimed, a little too eagerly, as he bolted up from one of the lobby chairs.

We included him in our group for that day and the next. He came with us on a hike and a visit to a wildlife reserve. He acted like he was going to travel with us forever but failed to gel in our group dynamic. He offered to make us dinner reservations. We told him we had other plans. He appeared hurt, more so than the situation warranted. Luckily, we didn't see him the following day at all.

The day after that, my friends and I boarded a bus for the next spot on our self-created itinerary. It was someone in our group's birthday, and we were all in good spirits. Our bus trip was a longer one, and it took us nearly eleven hours to reach the next hotel. We arrived under darkness and agreed to meet up in the morning for breakfast.

At breakfast, a friend came to me and said, "Rebekah, did you invite Billy here?"

I turned around, unnerved. "Billy? He's here?"

And sure enough, there he was, waving from a large breakfast table. One he had obviously secured for the group. Our group. Meeting once is genuine, twice is co-incidence, but three times is a pattern. And, in this case, an unwelcome one.

Reluctantly, we sat with Billy at the table and engaged in awkward conversation. Without any prompting from me, my group stopped mentioning our future plans and our destinations in front of Billy and, instead, engaged in benign subjects like the weather, the beauty that was the hotel, and our luck that the bacon was crispy.

The group ate quickly and left. I lingered. A friend said to me as she left the table, "Come to my room after." She knew I was going to clear the air with Billy.

"Why did your plans change again?" I asked him.

"I came to see you. I knew that you would miss me."

I explained to Billy, diplomatically, that he may have misinterpreted our time together. I told him that I en-joyed meeting him and our personal experience. But, I said, pointedly, the remainder of our travels were in-tended to be with me and my group. I said I couldn't stop him from traveling wherever he wanted or staying where he wished, but joining our group was no longer an op-tion.

I paused for a reaction.

Billy didn't speak. I was confident my message had been clear, so I rose from the table and said, "Thank you for understanding. Have a great rest of your trip."

But then Billy spoke.

"I think we belong together. I'm not going to give up that easily. I knew when I saw you in that market that you were the one for me."

Unnerved by his delusion, I sat back down and looked directly into his pleading eyes.

"Billy, let's be clear," my voice becoming harsher, "I am not interested in seeing you. Not now at this hotel, or at any stop on my future trip. Please respect that."

Unfortunately, Billy didn't respect that.

At our next destination, we scoured the resort carefully. There were no signs of Billy. Days went by. Still no Billy. And then we let our guard down.

As we loaded our gear on the bus, bound for the desert, ready for the last leg on our journey, I spotted him in the parking lot. He was leaning against a car not far away, staring right at me. I quickly told the others. We were collectively stunned. Why wasn't this guy getting the message?

One of the guys in our group walked over, and I watched as Billy jumped in the car, refusing to open the door or crack the window. Through the closed window, my friend tried to tell Billy that he was not welcome and that he had to stop following us.

Instead of acknowledging my friend, Billy sped off in his rental car.

Afterward, we boarded our bus. I was deeply embarrassed and apologetic to the gang. I had brought this upon us and wished I could have taken back the mediocre sex that led to his attachment. They consoled me and were incredibly understanding. By the first rest stop we were happily chatting and making our arrival plans. Thankfully, we did not see Billy again.

What I hadn't known at the time, was that Billy, while I had not been looking, had copied down my home address off my luggage tag. To my dismay, waiting for me when I got home was a long, twenty-five-page handwritten letter spelling out his love for me. He included his home address in the letter but I did not respond.

Weeks went by and strange packages addressed to me started arriving. I received a fridge magnet from the country where I had met Billy and a postcard from another part of that country, picturing the market where he had first seen me. It was entirely blank except for my address.

Then fresh flowers arrived one day with a card that said, "Love, Me."

I wrote a brief note to the return address that came with the original letter. I knew Billy had lived with his mother when I met him and likely still did. I addressed it to her directly and hoped she would get her hands on it before he did.

I appealed to her sense of compassion as a woman and explained his stalking behavior without disparaging her son. I told her I sincerely hoped she would interfere before I had to get the authorities involved. Not that I really understood how I would do that.

Months passed. There were no mysterious packages, no further communications. A year later, when I received a blank postcard depicting the town I lived in, I moved.

Thankfully, Billy never followed the moving van.

38

NUMBER FIFTY-NINE

Guy number fifty-nine was an asshole masquerading as a nice guy. We met at a local pub. He saw me answering emails on my phone one evening after work. He said, "I bet I'm more interesting than whatever is on your phone."

I said, "Prove it," and put my phone down, intrigued by the novel pickup line.

We chatted for over an hour. I knew the bartender and had included her in our conversation. After our chat, he and I didn't exchange numbers and went our separate ways.

About a week later, he appeared at a bar across town that was hosting a "paints and pints" night that I happened to be attending. It was an evening where an artist, an extremely patient one, walks the group through the process of creating a "masterpiece" while the students sip drinks and become increasingly noncompliant.

I saw him right away when I entered the bar. He was not far from the entrance, pretending to read a local newspaper. I walked over and said hello.

"I was hoping to run into you here," he said. "I went to Brushes and Beers and Canvas and Cappuccino before I found the right event."

We laughed and spent about an hour together before I moved to the event room for the painting night. He asked for my number, but he never texted.

About three weeks later, I cruised by the bar where we'd first met. I wasn't expecting to see him and wasn't worried if I did—or didn't. As soon as I walked in, the bartender said, "Rebekah, you have mail."

Mail? In a bar? Clearly, I went there too often.

It was him, the one that I met, re-met, and lost. He wasn't there. But he'd left me something.

The note said: *I didn't put your number in my phone. I couldn't find it. Sorry. Let's go out, if you want. Jeff.* He included his number. The little note was folded into a tiny cube and the sides of the cube had colorful letters that spelled out my name.

I was flattered. I took a picture of it folded cube-style and another of the note flattened out with its many folds and crinkles. I thought it was romantic.

I texted him a few days later, playing it cool. I sent a rhyming text about a girl who found a note in a bar, a-bar-not-far, and whether he wanted to grab a beer and some cheer. It was lame but cute.

Apparently it hit its mark, because Jeff responded right away. He texted saying it was funny, and he was glad I got his note.

We arranged to meet and spent a couple of evenings a week together after the note: a movie, some dinners, meeting at the bar after work, and a quick sandwich at a roadside stand on an evening where we both had other plans.

I got to know about his life, his job, his family, his roots. We were about the same age and a song playing in a restaurant made us say, "Where were you when this song came out?"

I liked him.

The night he came to my house for dinner, our first sleepover. He arrived late. And he was acting odd and seemed a little pissed off. I wasn't sure what was going on. Then I figured out he was drunk—and had driven to my house.

Not cool.

When I brought it up, he brushed it off. Dinner continued as planned, and he devoured the food in minutes. We watched some comedic special on the couch and began kissing. I never offered him a drink.

We ended up in my bedroom around 9:00 p.m. It seemed sloppy and amateur. I compensated by taking the lead. He twisted around and moaned at times when neither was called for. He was clearly too drunk to participate.

I called a halt to the shenanigans. He seemed angry. He said he'd stopped at the bar "for a few" on his way here. That accounted for his lateness and his condition, but it also showed me a different side of note-writing man. He wanted to continue. Unsure, I agreed, giving him credit for confiding in me.

We tried a few more positions, switching styles a little more rapidly than I felt necessary and suddenly, after another failed attempt, he jumped out of bed, nearly smacking his head on the dresser next to the window.

"I'm outta here!" he proclaimed.

"What's wrong?" I asked, switching on the bedside lamp, while holding the sheet to cover me.

"I don't have time for this."

"Sorry??"

"This is just too pedestrian for me."

Pedestrian?

"What are you talking about?" I asked, fully under-standing the meaning of the word.

"You!" he yelled, fighting to get his legs in his pants. "You are boring in bed."

I remember saying, "Hey, I know you have been drink-ing and were having trouble..."

To which he replied, "I think if I had a better partner, it wouldn't have been a problem."

His pants were fully on now, but not zipped. He was struggling to put his arms in his shirt. It was inside out, with the sleeves folded in upon themselves. I watched, still shocked as his rant continued.

"I'm sure I will see you again at the bar. We can try again sometime if you want. Your call. But I don't think you will get any better."

Wow. Did he just say that?

I didn't see him out. In fact, I never left the bed at all. I let him leave, drunk and all, with his truck. Morally right or wrong, I didn't stop him.

The day after he left my house, I called three ex-boyfriends and asked, through tears, in a gasping voice, if I was bad in bed. Each one was completely bewildered at my inquiry. They all reassured me they had no complaints when they were with me. Whether it was pity or truth, it helped.

I did see Jeff at the bar, about a month later. I confronted him and told him he behaved poorly. I railed him for being late, drunk, and blaming me for his sexual lapse. Then I told him he couldn't treat women that way.

Jeff denied it all. He continued to defend his position that I was not sexy, nor was I "as advertised."

My voice faltered. I told him, "You know, you can't speak to people this way. We've all had sex with people who weren't our match. Bad sex, even. You don't get to offer commentary after it's over, like you are reviewing a play."

He looked at me in a condescending way: "I do if it was bad. And it was. And you should know that. The truth is important."

His truth, that is. My truth was that he was drunk, rude, and degrading. But I still cried when it happened and again when I confronted him that night.

I had pulled myself together and had gotten my mojo back, but when I ran into him at the bar, I wanted so badly for him to apologize. And his refusal to do so put me right back there, like it had just happened.

I left him in that bar. My quick departure, obviously showing that I had been hurt. It was six months before I saw him again while I was in a grocery store. It was too late to change course, as I saw him nearby in the meat section.

He said, "Hey, Rebekah," like we were friends.

"Hi," I said, wishing I'd ordered in.

"How's your summer going?" he asked and bumped his shopping basket into mine suggestively.

Were we doing this?

"My summer is great, Jack. I hope yours is, too, Jack. Good seeing you, Jack."

I said it calmly and with a wide smile. And then I casually moved away from the meats to the frozen foods. Still smiling, because I knew his name was Jeff.

39

NUMBER FIFTY-ONE

Guy number fifty-one was a complete gentleman. I debated whether he should get a number, since he was an almost-on-the-list-guy—a good one that got away. But he made an impression—a good one. So, I figured he should receive an honorary number at the very least.

The air was cold, and there was a decided mist coming off the heated pool that day. It was one of those infinity pools that flowed endlessly into the distance, or so it seemed. When I swam to the edge, I was aware of just how high up in the mountains I was, with snow-topped peaks all around me.

My flight had been delayed, almost four hours late, making it one of the last ones out of the airport that night. Suddenly, my long weekend in the mountains became shorter. My first full day consisted of a tricky run on the well-marked paths of the resort. Frost-covered leaves crunched under my running shoes. The swim was a peaceful prize.

The pool had a small cluster of inhabitants, two men and a woman chatting near the waterfall's edge. I joined the admiration of the view, standing at the pool wall a short distance from them. I overhead their discussion of a flight delay. Turns out it was the same flight I was on, so I joined their conversation. Although we were not complaining—no one could really complain in such a beautiful setting—we agreed that the delay was unfortunate.

I saw the group again after dinner. I was in the lobby, dressed in winter layers, ready for the hike to discover animal tracks and identify foliage. The three of them were clustered by the stone fireplace drinking from steaming mugs. One man in the group, Kurt, came forward and asked me about my plans after the hike. He had a strong accent. German, perhaps. We introduced ourselves, and the couple at the table waved as he gestured toward them. I waved back politely and agreed to join them when I returned.

But Kurt and his group were no longer there when my hiking troop returned to the resort. Stomping the snow off my boots and removing the scarf that I'd wrapped several times around my neck, I passed through the pine-filled lobby, heading for my room. And that's when I heard my name called as I approached the elevator.

It was Kurt.

"Join me for a drink by the fire?"

I was pleasantly surprised and turned around to face him: "Sure, let me change first."

I was basically stalling so I could get out of my wool-lies and put on something more feminine and run a brush through my matted hair.

By the fire, he drank a dark-colored beer out of a glass that he sipped very slowly without refilling. I didn't recognize the brand on the empty can that was partially crumpled on the table. When the waiter came, I chose a hot chocolate to defrost my fingers and followed it up with the same beer Kurt was having, based on his recommendation. We talked about the resort, his travel companions and their travel plans. He shared they were work colleagues and staying for the same duration as me. After that, he said they were returning to Germany, which was home for all of them.

Kurt said that he and his team traveled regularly for work. He described his occupation as "customer service related." He wasn't being evasive. I understood how Europeans don't necessarily identify themselves by their occupation as many North Americans do, so I changed the subject.

I told him about my plans for the following day, which included a much-anticipated appointment in the spa. Kurt smiled and said his included sleeping in, something he said rarely happened.

We talked until close to midnight. We were both leaving the next day. I was starting to lament that the short retreat was speedily ending.

At the elevator we discovered we were both staying on the same floor. At the turn in the hallway where he was to go right to 309 and I was to go left to 301, he asked if he could kiss me. Kiss me. I'd never have anyone ask permission like that before. Frankly, I was impressed.

The kiss was sweet. Like a long kiss with a small peck at the end—sort of like a goodbye.

"If I don't see you tomorrow, have a safe trip home," Kurt said.

"You too, Kurt."

* * *

At the airport, thoroughly relaxed from my spa experience, I had already checked my luggage and was waiting in line for airport security when I saw the couple traveling with Kurt. And then I saw Kurt—all of them wearing airline uniforms.

"Hi Rebekah," Kurt said to me, looking stylish in his jacket with epaulettes and wearing a pilot's cap.

"You're a pilot? And you're flying today?"

"Yes," he smiled.

"Are you flying my plane?" I asked, forgetting that he had said Germany was his destination.

"No. I got you here, though." (And now I hoped I hadn't said anything negative about the flight during that inaugural conversation at the pool).

At that moment, the work-colleague comment and the regular travel made sense, along with the reluctance to share his occupation.

"Thank you," I managed, with a smile.

"Glad I did," he said as he strolled toward his gate.

And then he was gone.

All three of them were gone. Along with many others in similar uniforms from varying airlines, fast-tracking through security, while I was still putting my shoes back on, wishing he were flying my plane, so I could see him again when we landed.

40

NUMBER SIXTY-ONE

I met guy number sixty-one when he handed me a glass of champagne with a wink. By day five of my stay, he had his own key to my room.

He was native to Saint Lucia and was the bar manager at the wellness resort in my newfound paradise. I was staying for seven days. I'd just returned from a run on the beach. I'd rinsed off most of the sand that clung to me but still looked like I'd been adrift in a dingy for three weeks. Leave it to me to have my hair plastered to my face, courtesy of the sea air and sweat-soaked clothes, when I meet a handsome bartender.

I had hydrated with water on the run and was passing by the bar on my way to my room to shower. Jayden, according to his name tag, was pouring champagne into glasses on a tray and set to deliver them to a rowdy group of women by the nearby pool.

"How was your run?" he asked.

"Sweaty. I now know what it's like to be on the surface of the sun."

He smiled and placed a glass of water on the edge of the bar for me, momentarily stopping his flute-filling duties. He also pulled one glass of champagne off the tray, handed it to me, and winked, "Your reward."

I drank the water. And the champagne. Enjoying both equally. I saw Jayden's frame grow smaller as he, and his full tray, headed for the pool.

The resort marketed itself as an opportunity to heighten or maintain physical fitness and spiritual awareness. I'd never considered a vacation where I'd be registered in endurance-building classes or have a set workout regimen. It was day two, and I was already starting to ache—my late-thirties body registering complaints.

The ladies by the pool had obviously chosen the "leave us alone" package. I would have become envious of them, but my packed schedule didn't allow time for wallowing. I was late for ballet class, something I had not attempted since I was too young to put on my own ballet flats. My options for that timeslot had been ballet basics or introduction to drumming. So, I chose ballet, since I didn't see "drink your body weight" or "sleep all day" on the menu.

I squeezed in a nap on a comfy lounger on the shady side of the pool after ballet class. A solo in Swan Lake was not in my future, but I enjoyed the stretching, posing, and breathing techniques. I signed up for another session later in the week, surprising myself.

The nap helped me recharge before racquetball. At the court, the instructor was surprised to hear I'd never played, so he explained the rules to me. I held my own for forty minutes, stopping twice to mop my face and dry my hands. The racquet was repeatedly slipping from my sweaty palms. Not long after our last water break, I took a nasty rebound shot to the upper thigh.

My Lycra shorts had offered little in the way of protection from the tiny ball, and I yelped in pain when it hit.

The instructor was immediately apologetic and pulled me aside. He had me fill in the necessary incident form while he wrapped an icepack around my leg.

"Please wait here so our first-aid supervisor can have a look."

"I'm OK. That's OK...," I protested, fearing I would be stuck in the gym's hallway for the rest of the day.

"He is on his way. Please wait."

I was embarrassed by all the fuss. It turned out the bar manager I'd seen earlier also performed the role as first-aid supervisor. He recognized me immediately. Once again, I was sweaty and not at my best.

"You again!" he said with a smile, as we introduced ourselves.

He asked the requisite questions and looked at my leg, where a sizable lump had formed. He spoke with my racquetball coach. Was that French? I hoped the instructor wasn't catching hell for what happened to me.

It wasn't anyone's fault. I simply didn't know enough to get out of the way of the ball.

My wilting ice bag was exchanged for a fresh one, and I was helped to my feet. The group that had gathered around me dissipated, and Jayden offered to walk me to my room. I agreed, although I felt it was unnecessary. In the breezeway leading to the cluster of rooms in my section, I thanked him for his help. He joked that I had earned myself a rest and said he would give me a new ice pack later at the bar.

"The bar has the ice. And the champagne," he smiled, meeting my eyes.

41

Other than my throbbing leg, the rest of me was fine. I showered and slipped into a bathing suit and sundress. I didn't want any clothing touching my leg and felt that some time at the pool was in order. Using the resort's scheduling app on my phone, I swapped out that evening's yoga class for a nature photography seminar.

The pool gave me the tranquility I desired. The rowdy group of women were no longer there, likely attending one of the activities offered at the resort. A few couples were scattered around, and I could see therapists conducting a couple's massage in a thatched roof hut where the pool pathway curved toward the beach.

This resort did not have the customary pool drink service or the smell of fast-food grease wafting in the air. With a focus on wellness, you sacrificed oily pleasures for healthy ones. I went to the smoothie bar and reviewed the options. A four-page menu of smoothies. Who knew? I chose something with plenty of healthy ingredients, while ensuring it would still taste like a smoothie and not like a garden.

At my pool lounger, another staff member brought me a new ice pack. He asked whether I was feeling better and if I needed medical attention. I assured him I was fine and thanked him for his concern.

He nodded and said, "I will let Jayden know."

At 6:00 p.m. trays of shots were circulated poolside. Most of the loungers were occupied, as the daytime sessions had ended and the evening ones had not yet begun. Dinnertime was a well-respected break in the schedule. I could see about ten staff members with trays fanning out and individuals on loungers leaning forward to choose their selection. I removed my earbuds to hear what was being said.

After getting a glass, we were all instructed to hold them up in cheers to one another and to drink in tandem. I'd chosen the only option containing alcohol on the tray, something fruity with a hint of cinnamon. After the toast, the glasses were then collected, and the waiters left with their trays. The activity was so quick, so delicately orchestrated, that if someone had not been paying attention, it could easily have been overlooked.

Jayden then approached me carrying two small glasses. He sat at the foot of the unoccupied lounger beside me and offered me the glass that held the drink I had just drunk. The contents of his glass were green and thicker, most likely nonalcoholic.

"To the brave girl," he toasted in a thick accent.

We clinked glasses and drank. Jayden asked about the sessions I'd attended that day and my upcoming schedule. He gave high praise to that evening's photography course, a last-minute substitution. He expressed concern over my planned level of exertion in the coming days, specifically cautioning that the rock climbing and Tae Bo might not be wise. He suggested I consider replacing these with less-strenuous alternatives. I compromised by pulling out my phone and moving them to later in the week. This left a hole in my schedule. The entire following day was clear.

"There is plenty to do at the resort, even without classes," he offered. "You can go for a ride on a sailboat or kayak or just relax. I have to return to work. Please enjoy your evening, Rebekah. I hope to see you later after the evening performance."

Then he shook my hand and looked me right in the eye. Before releasing my hand, I studied him carefully, noting his eyes were beautiful.

I ate dinner quickly, as I had lingered at the pool longer than intended. It was a simple meal: a few salads topped with hearty proteins. I hadn't eaten that many vegetables in years. I wished I could have the healthy chef permanently in my own home, knowing I would undoubtedly return to my old ways once I left the resort.

The photography course lived up to Jayden's praise. It provided examples and tips on how to use your phone as a professional camera. We learned about capturing nature's beauty using the sun's angle, how to accent colors in shade, and how to best frame a subject. I was very glad that my fate caused me to switch courses. So glad, in fact, that I became a vocal endorsement to other guests that week.

The class was an hour long, letting us out just as people were gathering in the outdoor pavilion for that evening's entertainment. It was described as "hidden talents of the staff." We saw surprise acts such as the tennis instructor who juggled, the yoga instructor who sang, and the groundskeeper who played piano. Less surprising demonstrations included the talents of the entertainment staff, who, as expected, were already entertaining by nature.

By then the swelling on my leg had gone down, and it no longer felt hot to the touch. I'd stopped using the ice packs when the heat went away. The only remnant from the mishap was a significant bruise that was starting to form. Unless I touched the bruised area, I was no longer in pain.

I left the show shortly before the closing number. With no strenuous sessions arranged the following day, I'd planned to have a few cocktails that evening. I was also hoping to run into Jayden again. I'd detected a spark between us but was unsure if his camaraderie was genuine interest or merely due to my injury and his role in providing aid.

I joined a few people I'd met the previous day around the bar. We each recounted our exercise woes and itemized aches in places that hadn't hurt the week before. Someone mentioned a craving for nachos and lamented they weren't on the healthy menu, as I sipped from my glass and nonchalantly scanned the staff for Jayden.

No luck.

As the crowds gathered, now released from the entertainment pavilion, I left the bar and walked back to my room, glass in hand. I stopped to read the activity board for the following day, noting opportunities that both me and my injured leg could participate in.

"Rebekah?"

The voice startled me.

"How is your leg?"

I turned to see Jayden carrying bags of ice and what appeared to be a bottle of mixer under each arm.

"I think I will keep it...seems a shame to cut it off after all of these years," hoping that my humor translated well.

He chuckled. "That's good. Are you leaving already?"

"I am. It was really busy out there."

"See you tomorrow, I hope."

And that's when I knew I wasn't imagining the connection. This was not just about my leg, but the rest of me, too.

42

The next day I went kayaking and catamaran sailing, following Jayden's recommendations. I enjoyed the water activities and was relieved we concluded before lunch, so I could freshen up a bit before heading to the common area. Knowing that Jayden was signaling he wanted something less platonic, I wanted to look my best before he saw me next.

That afternoon, full from another healthy meal, I stationed myself on the beach. On a trip to the restroom, I waved at Jayden, who was across the room, behind the bar. He motioned me toward him and asked about my day and my plans for later. He said he'd finish at 4:00 p.m. and, although not permitted to use the resort's pool or engage in the activities, he was allowed on the beach, if he was not obvious about it.

I nodded and told him where my beach chair was, thinking he likely already knew.

Jayden surprised me when he approached in his street clothes not long after his shift ended. I don't know why I had expected to see him in his uniform, as if he wore it 24/7. It was great to see that with his change of clothes, the formality of the server/guest relationship also disappeared. We walked along the beach together, less as a romantic stroll, and more to escape viewing range of his colleagues and staff.

As we talked, I learned he was a little older than me, divorced like I was, and into athletic pursuits. I cautioned him that this week was not a normal one for me and that I was not prone to trying a new sport every day or sweating it out in the gym constantly. He complimented me on my willingness to try new things. I complimented him on his position at the resort after he explained it was hard to rise above entry-level jobs there.

Beyond the resort's stretch of beach, where a different color of beach umbrella bearing a new resort name became the norm, Jayden took my hand. We walked the remainder of the beach, right to the rocky outcrop, asking random questions of each other. And when the beach ended, we kissed.

I initiated it. Taking my cue from him, I deduced he only was comfortable out of sight of anyone he knew. I didn't interpret this as he was married, or he was ashamed of me. I fully understood the value of his job and how breaking the rules would jeopardize it. I pulled his hand that I was holding behind my back, creating a hug and as he moved closer, and then I planted a soft kiss on his lips. He was taller and the sand made us somewhat unsteady, so a bit of my kiss landed on his chin, causing me to giggle.

We sat for a while in a pedal boat that had been moved onto the shoreline. As we talked about our very different lives, I became envious of his and he began wishing he had mine.

We agreed that our envy was romanticized, since anywhere you lived there were sacrifices, jobs, bills, chores you hated, people you didn't get to see as often as you wanted, and things you just never seemed to find time to do.

"We are very alike, you and I," Jayden said—words I'd already thought to be true.

We saw each other again the next day and the next. I continued with my workshops, narrowly surviving an intense spin class, modeling a mug out of clay, and finally trying the rock wall, after postponing it from earlier in the week.

We made the most of our days together, stealing scraps of time after his shifts before he made his long journey home. We talked when other guests were occupied, and I walked with him when he carried items between locations at the resort.

After our second day together, I snuck him into my room. I ventured ahead, and he walked gingerly along the outskirts of the path, out of view of the many hidden cameras at the resort. I knew the extreme risk he was taking to be with me and for that reason I felt a more immediate bond to him.

The next morning I discreetly gave him a key to my room when I handed back some cocktail napkins at the bar that had scattered in a sudden breeze. To no surprise, he and I managed a brief encounter later that afternoon, before dinner, each arriving separately from different paths on the resort property.

And the next day, when I stopped by my room hastily to change after a class, I found flower petals arranged across my floor in the shape of a smiley face. I knew it was not the work of the housekeeping staff. I pulled out my phone and took several snapshots, choosing my favorite as my new Instagram profile pic.

43

At other resorts, when I had occasion to meet men, I knew our time together was limited and that always gave me an understanding of when, if not how, things would end. I actually prided myself on my detachment.

With Jayden, however, it was the first time I'd seriously contemplated asking someone to come with me. Another ballet class and an afternoon of lawn bowling and croquet did not change my mind. When I saw Jayden that evening, freshly showered and sitting on the love seat in my room, I mentioned it. I just outright asked if he would consider leaving with me.

At first he laughed. Then he realized I was serious. At which I tried to pretend I had been joking all along. He looked at me tenderly and told me what I had already guessed: His life was in Saint Lucia. He said that resort life was just fantasy and that as much as we had in common, one of us would ultimately be giving up everything to be with the other.

I hated that it was true.

We made love afterward, and he slipped out while I was sleeping. And even though I knew the next day was his day off, and we wouldn't get to see each other, the resort lacked its previous shine. I missed him and wondered if he felt the same.

And then my last day came. I had a late flight and was sipping a smoothie on a swing on the manicured grounds of the resort. I reflected on the past week, now almost over. I'd learned new sports, embraced different challenges, and gained perspective.

But I did crave French fries. Especially the ones covered in cheese.

I didn't see Jayden. I tried not to envision he was avoiding me. But, in truth, I was pretty certain that was the case.

With my bag collected and my name checked off the list, I boarded the minivan for the trip to the airport. Before getting in the van, I'd glanced around the reception area hoping to say goodbye to him, even though I knew he likely wouldn't be able to say anything in front of other staff anyhow. But there was no sign of Jayden. While I understood he was working, his absence stung.

As the van pulled away from the resort, I looked around, noticing every occupant sported a varying degree of new tan and exhaustion. The open windows let in a soft, balmy breeze. The group was quiet and some people napped.

About ten minutes into the thirty-minute ride to the airport, the van pulled into a rest stop, and the driver told the group we were making a quick stop and that everyone should remain seated. I presumed we were getting gas for the van.

My name was called by the driver as he opened the sliding side door. I waved and said, "That's me." And behind him, in the distance, was Jayden.

I jumped out of the van, nearly knocking over the driver, rushing into Jayden's arms. We kissed in full view of the departing guests. Tears stung my eyes. He whispered softly in my ear. We knew we were out of time. We kissed again and I boarded the van, as every occupant watched. Some clapped, while others seemed pretty annoyed by the unscheduled stop.

I softly repeated to myself what he had whispered to me just moments ago: "Goodbye, brave girl."

And while our departure was bittersweet, I smiled and wiped the tears away that were trickling down my cheeks. I *was* brave. More than he knew. Brave for putting myself out there in the first place. And brave for knowing I could do it again.

PART THREE: MASON

44

Mason, who had never called or responded to my texts, returned the next day. Olivia heard his key in the lock while I was in the bedroom grabbing a sweater. Mason had nodded to her soundlessly when he came in the living room and she gestured upstairs. He started up the stairs to find me as she arranged her rideshare and waited on the front porch, giving us the privacy we needed.

"Rebekah?"

I heard his voice over the running water in the bathroom, as I splashed cold water on my puffy face, swollen from crying. I approached him, still carrying the towel.

I could tell from his face that he was not OK. His eyes appeared vacant, and he kept touching his lips, like they were itchy. He seemed nervous.

He had gone to my condo in the city, he explained. He still had the key on his key ring and knowing the new owners were not taking possession until the following weekend, he went there to think, alone.

"Without any furniture? Or food?"

"I ordered in and sat on the balcony set you were leaving for the new owners. I slept on the floor."

He had gotten my texts, our friends' texts, and had noted my increased anxiety with each message. He apologized for not responding and said he was sorry that I worried.

I moved forward to hug him and he stiffened. His hug in return was mechanical, not enveloping like usual.

We talked for hours. He owned most of the dialogue.

He quickly asked why his name wasn't on the list if I had only made it over the past week. He raised his voice slightly, covering it with a cough, when he asked about my previous marriages.

He mumbled "three or is it four?" when he inquired about the number of men I had lived with before.

And I think I saw tears forming in his eyes when he asked, holding my gaze for the first time since coming home, "Were you ever serious about me?"

I noticed he kept using the past tense.

He used words like "you lied," and "you hid your past." All of his accusations were expected. His voice alternated from a hoarse whisper to a pleading tone. For as many questions as he asked, he answered them himself. His conversation was mostly one-sided, with me bearing witness.

I let him speak. I didn't interrupt, correct his assumptions, or offer my truth. I knew he couldn't hear me right now. He would hear the words, but not their meaning.

The afternoon turned to night.

His emotional state surprised me. He was always so steady, someone who faced uncertainty and unexpected detours with methodical, rational countermeasures. At one point he sat in the bedroom chair, near the dresser filled with my freshly unpacked clothes, and said, "I have to think you made the list *hoping* I would find it."

With that, he rose and we began to get ready for sleep, in silence. He left the room to brush his teeth, and I pulled back the sheets on the bed. When he finished in the bathroom, I went in to do the same. The love note on the mirror from that previous morning was now smudged, and the white hand towel had blue marker across the front. Returning to the bedroom, I found the light out and Mason curled on his side, as far from the middle of the bed as possible. I crawled in, giving him space, feeling every bit of the distance between us.

***

Sleep came quickly, and I awoke in the morning alone in the bedroom, with his side of the bed fully made, initially making me question whether he had been there at all. I didn't get up immediately, choosing instead to lie still and think about us and whether there still was an "us."

Mason and I had first met in a gas station convenience store, of all places. I had been on my way home from a friend's place one Saturday afternoon and had pulled in to fill up before returning to the city, where gas was much more expensive. While there, I grabbed the few essentials from my list, which were an odd assortment of products, like pickles and dental floss. I can't even remember what all the items were, but I do remem-

264

ber Mason had the exact same items in his basket. Right down to the brand of milk. We both approached the counter and as I placed my items up for scanning, he said, "Wait, are you doing my shopping for me?"

It was too coincidental not to have a conversation. We stood outside the store, bags in hand, talking for ages. We clicked. He asked for my number, and I wrote it on the store's receipt and watched him fold it and place it in his coat pocket.

He'd left me a voicemail by the time I reached my condo.

During our year together we spent most weekends in the city. We engaged in city events—festivals, theater openings, harborside fairs, and eclectic restaurants. I enjoyed his home and loved his cozy street with the mature trees and mailboxes at the curb. When we stayed at his place, we rode our bikes on parkland trails, fed ducks in man-made ponds, and tended to his fledgling vegetable garden. He was happy to make me new recipes while I set the table with elaborate centerpieces inspired from Pinterest.

Where our life in the city was fast-paced and vibrant, our time in the suburbs was relaxed and serene. Our homes reflected our personalities. We enjoyed our time in each other's world but recognized our own preferences and customs.

I met his family and was introduced to his friends early on, as social and work event invitations were frequently extended. Mason met my family about three months before the move, unintentionally delayed due to logistics and distance.

We were romantic and sensual with each other, striking the right balance of connection. Our relationship hosted no arguments, no loud differing of opinions, no slamming-door standoffs or other relationship drama. Past the age of needing parental approval, or youth-driven angst over money issues, we found contentment in our peaceful partnership. The decision to move in with Mason was easy. I didn't need to make a pro/con list, as I had in the past. I was in love with my heart and my head. With my other relationships behind me, and the gift of full hindsight, I knew Mason was the one.

45

Which is why it ultimately surprised me when it didn't work out. Mason and me. After three weeks of polite cohabitation and saying "oops, sorry" when our arms accidentally touched while reaching for the coffee mugs in the cupboard and days where we prepared meals in relative silence, exchanging only minimal dialogue, our time had come to an end.

A few times, Mason would brighten up telling me a story, referencing someone from work I knew, and just as fast, a cloud would come over him, as if reminding him that he wasn't supposed to show happiness. I cannot count the number of times I said, "Mason, let's talk." And we would. But it always ended the same way. Me asking him what I could do and how we could fix this.

During those weeks, I did manage to express the salient points of my side of the story. My first marriage was a brief blunder, it hadn't even registered as noteworthy, but he insisted it counted. I pleaded that this was all in the past and I had grown beyond that. But Mason was resolute in his determination to hold this over me.

Olivia showed less compassion in her texts to me. *He's acting like a child. So you have a past, who doesn't? Is he upset that you lied or that you aren't a virgin?*

Her texts, although brash, were valid. I cleaned up her sentiments and asked Mason her questions, as well as my own. I often wondered, was his disappointment in the misinformation or my past in general?

His regular response was, "I just can't explain. I'm not sure about anything."

Olivia, a lawyer, repeatedly asked to come to the house and lobby on my behalf. But I told her my relationship was already crowded enough with me, Mason, and the men on the list.

I came home from work on a Thursday, a bit later than usual, and a savory smell greeted me as I set down my belongings just inside the front door. I could hear music wafting from the kitchen and walking closer I saw the candles on the table already lit.

Mason appeared to be his usual self.

"Wine?" he asked, opening the cupboard and grabbing a glass for each of us.

"Sure."

I was both surprised and impressed with the display. The preparation must have taken him all afternoon. And the lobster bisque was exquisite.

It was during the main course, a stuffed chicken breast with cashew coating that Mason calmly said, between bites, "Rebekah, I can't do this any longer."

Initially mistaking that he meant he couldn't be mad any longer, I felt instant relief and smiled.

His next words were, "So, I arranged at the bank to refund your co-payment on the house and the money should be in your account by the end of the week." And then he added, "You are welcome until you find somewhere else to stay, although I'm sure you will likely prefer to crash with Olivia."

I didn't finish chewing the mouthful of juicy chicken. I didn't get to savor the cheese and spinach center. Instead, I washed it down whole with a slurp of wine and left the table. Heartbroken.

Without rage or fanfare, Mason helped me box up all of my stuff the next day. We spoke on innocuous topics, surprisingly able to form cordial conversation. You would think I would have been angry, lashing out with hateful comments, trying to pain him as he had me. But I knew pain had already been inflicted on him. I'd hurt him with my lie of omission. And he was not able to move past it. But I couldn't shut off my love for him that easily.

I'd read a quote once, "Relationships last only until someone wants something different. Eventually someone wants more, or someone wants less. It's whether the more or the less can be found with each other that decides."

With each box that was closed and taped, I was painfully aware that just a short time ago, I had been doing the exact same thing, but with the cheerful anticipation of being with Mason. And now I was packing to leave Mason. I saw my hands packing, but it was like they belonged to someone else. I wasn't really conscious of my participation. I didn't want to leave. It seemed that in this situation, I wanted more and Mason wanted less. Less of my past. Or less of me?

My phone buzzed as Olivia texted me from the curb. Once again, it was moving day.

46

EPILOGUE

Every single one of the encounters, the dates, the sexual experiences haven't all been exceedingly memorable, but I do indeed remember them all.

There was guy number fifty-six who decided that I traveled too much and said he had no interest in leaving the country. He lasted twelve weeks, sealing his fate at the time of the conversation.

There was a guy who revealed on date number one that he was obsessed with an impending apocalypse. He kept a food shelter and had fabricated a water distillery in his garage. He was fearful of all forms of public transit and felt that a tsunami would kill all beings, everywhere, who lived on any coastline. He claimed cell phones gave the government ammunition to kill you. After hearing all this, I excused myself between dinner and dessert, secretly paid the waitress, and exited the restaurant through the kitchen.

And there was the Abercrombie & Fitch model that my friends set me up with when were out one evening.

While I was in the washroom, they asked him to approach me and scripted a wildly flattering compliment to repeat. He obliged and ironically we hit it off, despite the false introduction. He became number fifty-eight. I only knew he was a model when I saw a life-size cardboard cutout of him in a clothing store window the following month.

There was also the security guard with a limp, introduced to me by a friend. He worked at her office building. After date number five, I realized he was crushing on my friend and not at all interested in me.

And many others. And the encounters weren't just for sex. Just the happenstance of meeting a man, enjoying a shared connection, and being wanted was enough to temporarily satisfy that inner yearning to connect.

Some men I have stayed in touch with. Whereas, others I have known only for hours. I am typically the one in my group of friends that ends up in a long embrace with the waiter after a catered cocktail party, munching on pizza with the movers after my belongings are unloaded, or exchanging contact details with the tour operator at the end of a trip.

I enjoy meeting others and am very aware of men.

***

I have always been a very positive person. For as long as I can remember I have turned hardships into opportunities or blindly ignored the shit that fate handed out. But don't mistake that for naivety. I fully get that life sometimes doesn't go my way—mostly because of choices I have made and sometimes because of things I didn't see coming.

There are days I imagine I have a theme song oversee-ing my world, like my walk-on-music, that plays while I strive forward in my day. It fuels my courage and gives energy to my step.

Some days I have regrets. Those days the music doesn't play.

Leaving someone is hard. Being left is even harder. I have seen both sides. And I am not without reflection. There were partnerships that I was too immature for, ones I wish I could have a do-over, and a very small few that I wish I never had. Even the bad ones, or the ones that ended too soon aren't necessarily regrettable. Those were the ones that taught me strength or made me who I am today.

For some relationships, I wasn't strong enough to leave. For others, I wasn't strong enough to stay.

Most of my friends are half of a couple. For a handful, it is their first love and there are kids, pets, and houses with beautiful yards. I follow them on social media, and we see each other as often as we can. Other friends are on their second, or third, marriage or other such long-term commitment. They seem as equally content.

Only a handful of my friends are single, like me. And we're at different stages in life. One is satisfied to spend time with her children and isn't seeking any relationship commitments. One claims she is too old to date and recently moved into her daughter's home. We joke that she will find someone before any of the rest of us.

And, until not long ago, I maintained that I just hadn't found my person. That he was out there. That I would find him one day. But after losing Mason, I've modified that.

I don't necessarily believe there is just *one* person for everybody. I believe there are *many* people we can connect with on different levels: meaningful hugs, laughs with strangers, or sexual trysts. It depends on timing, circumstances, and our willingness to make it happen.

I am also a realist. And I know that the odds just aren't in my favor.

One of my friends, in an attempt to console me after breaking up with Mason, said I will meet my forever person during my travels, and I'll move to some foreign land. My rebuttal has always been that I'm such a moving target, how could he find me? It's like if you ever get lost in a forest as a kid, you are taught to stay put and hug a tree. I don't hug trees well. I am always in motion.

So, there is a good chance he and I may have already been near each other but chose different lines for the commuter train or faced opposite directions while pumping gas and never caught each other's eye.

I've asked my friends, "Why do you think I haven't met my person?" Answers vary. Some claim it is fate's trick. Others think I want it too badly, which reflects in my behavior. And one said I'm "too giving to other people," and don't give enough to myself.

I have valued their opinions. But they have brought me no closer to finding him. And that's why I have decided to be happy alone. Just in case *alone* is my endgame.

Alone doesn't mean lonely.

It means making a life for yourself that doesn't necessarily include a partner. I have lots of friends and some family. I travel and socialize a great deal. And I won't stop the sexual excursions. I've had oodles of fun being in love and in like in my life, but I haven't used up my fair share of relationships.

I'm not done.

I do know I struggle with goodbyes. You might think I would be hardened to them. But I think the number of goodbyes I have endured has made me weak for their emotion. I cry when friends depart. I sob in airports and act sullen when driving home after well-attended dinner parties. I do not handle Sundays well, and I'd rather skip the formal debrief when ending a relationship.

And if I am lucky enough to find him, the guy for me, I will know he's the one right away. We won't play games or wait to call. Maybe he will pick up the boarding pass I drop at the airport gate, right as I'm getting ready to hand it to the attendant. Or he will be in the checkout line behind me at the store and joke that I have three items over the limit allowed for that lane.

He could even be a person who I already know, but we just haven't connected on that level.

But he will be funny. And *nice*. And *kind*.

And, God willing, there will be champagne...

Leighton Geller grew up accustomed to farm life in rural America. She left the Midwest for the first time ever, to attend college on the west coast. A few weeks after graduation she met her future husband, a man she has shared her life with for over two decades.

Their travels provided the backdrops for this novel and her imagination created the rest, embellished from bits and pieces of the stories her single friends told her.

Leighton is grateful to seize each day with her partner in love, her grown daughter and several four legged family members. This is her first work of fiction.